SOT 4

Trail of the Isotopes

Ron Wootters

"SOT 4 – Trail of the Isotopes," by Ron Wootters. ISBN 978-1-60264-026-9.

Published 2007 by Virtualbookworm.com Publishing Inc., P.O. Box 9949, College Station, TX 77842, US. ©2007, Ron Wootters. All rights reserved. No part of this publication may be reproduced, stored in a retrieval system, or transmitted in any form or by any means, electronic, mechanical, recording or otherwise, without the prior written permission of Ron Wootters.

Manufactured in the United States of America.

To:

All US Intelligence and Armed Forces Personnel
Past, Present & Future.
Thank You.

Richard Helms

Central Intelligence Agency 1947 - 1973
Director Central Intelligence Agency
Deputy Director of Plans (DDP)

Office of Strategic Services (OSS) 1943 - 1945

To Date the Last CIA Director

Edited by:
Lisa DiGloria
Book Ink Editing
www.bookink.com

In Memory Of:

**All coalition personnel who lost their lives serving their countries in
Iraq or Afghanistan.**

Continued Special Thanks To The Medical Community:

Dr. Jon Walheim, MD. Internal Medicine

Rosemary, our families, and I are very fortunate to live in an area where we have access to such excellent medical care.

PROLOGUE

It was a very hot late summer day in Izmir, Turkey, but the occasional breeze coming in off the Mediterranean Sea made it tolerable for the shoppers and street merchants.

One man wearing a white suit didn't seem to be bothered by the heat as he strolled down Vasif Cinar then entered Kultupark at the end of the boulevard. The huge park contained an amusement park, zoo, restaurants, and was the site of the International Izmir Fair.

The man continued his stroll to the quiet gardens at the park for a meeting with a man that had arrived by train and should also be making his way to the gardens. Even though he stopped from time to time to take in the sights and to make sure he was not being followed, he was right on schedule.

Approaching the site that had been selected for the meeting, he noticed a man observing the flowers and plant life as he slowly moved around the garden area. Already knowing his contact from the old days, he did not hesitate in joining the man as he admired the beautiful tulips along the walkway.

"One tends to associate the tulip with Holland," the man in the white suit observed.

"That's true," the other man answered, "but the Turks glorified the tulip long before the Dutch, and it is still their national flower."

"Is that so," the other man said, as he shook his head in agreement.

As the two men continued walking and admiring the tulips, the man in white started talking about the real reason for the meeting. "I have a client who has a client that is in the market for some isotopes."

"For bomb making?" the other man asked.

"The requirement is for such a small amount, I don't think so."

"Then it's a personal thing?"

"Maybe."

"I don't want to know anymore, do I?" was the next question.

"I wouldn't," he answered.

"I am not directly involved with the operation, but I could broker a deal for what you require," the man continued. "How long are you staying in Izmir?"

"I can stay for one week," he answered.

"The operation isn't in this country, but it's close. A week should be enough time to make contact and set up a meeting."

"If we come to an agreement, will I be able to take delivery in another country?" the man in white asked.

"I'm sure that can be arranged, for a price," was the confirmation.

"How can I be sure these people are handling the radioactive material in a safe manner?"

"My guess is for the amount and type of isotopes you require, it shouldn't be very dangerous."

"That didn't answer my question," the man in the white suit pursued.

"Well, I understand they have transported radioactive material in the past and I haven't seen anything in the press about it, have you?"

"No, but your answers are not giving me a high degree of confidence."

The two men continued their tour of the tulips and their conversation about the safe handling of the isotopes.

Chapter 1

Gil Dunn, president of Van Corcoven Firearms Company, was on the company jet halfway across the Atlantic on his way to Belgium. The trip was twofold. One, a surprise inspection of the manufacturing facility at Herstal and two, a meeting with Rene one of his associates from the days when he was Deputy Direction of Operations at the CIA.

After leaving the Agency, Gil never really got out of the Intelligence business and maintained a working relationship with Rene over the years. This working relationship was kicked into high gear in 2001 after Gil was asked to become a board member of an anti-terrorist group that was being formed in the private sector. Rene never questioned the increase in activity, but knew Dunn had to be involved in some sort of counterterrorism activity.

Gil and Rene had always communicated via secure phone, but this time, Rene requested they meet in person. Considering the fact that Rene was a very cool customer and not prone to panic, Gil immediately made arrangements for the trip.

———————

Dunn felt pleased as he navigated his rented BMW to Maastricht, a town just over the border in the Netherlands. The manufacturing facility had absolutely no advanced notice of his arrival or surprise inspection, yet everything was running smoothly. He was pleased, but not surprised. They had a good management team in place and all the workers took great pride in their work and finished products.

After Gil entered the city limits of Maastricht, he pulled to the curb, removed a city map from his inside pocket, and unfolded it. After discovering his present location, he checked the written directions he had prepared then continued to the restaurant where Rene would be waiting.

Navigating through the streets of Maastricht didn't seem to be that difficult, but in years past, Gil had to navigate through Washington, DC, and if you could find your way around there, you had a pretty good chance anywhere else on the planet.

After about ten minutes, a wrong turn, and some foul language, Dunn arrived at his destination. He didn't park at or near the restaurant, but rather drove past and parked about a block down the street. After taking a quick look around, he got out of the car and walked back toward his destination. *I'm starting to act as if it's the old days,* Dunn thought, as he approached the restaurant.

It was a little early for the dinner crowd and a maitre d' wasn't on duty yet when Gil entered the establishment. As he looked around, a voice inquired, "Old habits are hard to break, aren't they?"

As Dunn turned around, a big smile appeared on his face. They had many conversations on the phone over the years, but hadn't seen each other for a long time and he was happy to see his old friend. "How are you, my friend," Gil inquired, as he offered his right hand.

"I am well. It is good to see you again," Rene answered, as the two men clasped hands then embraced.

The two men had a lot of history between them. When Dunn was in the field for the first time, he ran across Rene in Naples, Italy. After some posturing, then some checking, both men discovered they were on the same side and both were rookies. Rene in French Intel and Gil at CIA. Discovering they had the same assignment, they decided instead of butting heads, they would join forces and both were successful on their first assignment.

Since they both worked for the west, the two collaborated, helped each other whenever they could and at least once saved the others life.

"We have a lot to catch up on," Gil finally said, as the emotions subsided.

"Yes, we do," Rene agreed, "but before we start reminiscing and hoisting a brew or two, I would like to tell you the reason I requested this meeting."

"Okay," Dunn said, as he shook his head in agreement.

Rene then led Gil to a table he had already reserved. After giving the waiter an order for two Ketel One martinis, the two sat back and surveyed the area for any unwanted ears. When they were satisfied, Rene leaned forward, rested both elbows on the table, and placed his hand in front of his mouth. After Gil did the same, Rene started to explain the reason for the meeting.

"I know our communications have been secure in the past, but the conversations have been very brief and to the point. This time, the issue is extremely sensitive and if we used the phone, too much info would be going out over the airways," Rene started.

"I understand," Gil agreed.

"I have a friend and working associate who was a former KGB officer and was in retirement until someone recruited him for a project. After the project was completed, he went back into retirement, only to be recruited for another project. I wouldn't want to say who keeps recruiting him, but he has been overheard saying, 'That fucking frog wouldn't let me retire.' Like the fucking Bolshevik really wants to," Rene added with a smile.

"I was wondering how you pulled off those last two things for me," Gil said in a very low voice.

"Like us," Rene continued, "the Bolshevik likes to keep up on what's happening in the Intel community and has come across some gossip. If true, it is a very serious situation. He has it from a good source that radioactive material was being sold and transported out of Russia or one of the old Soviet block countries and it isn't heading east."

"Is it weapons grade?" Gil inquired.

"I don't know," Rene replied, "but what we and everyone else in the world knows is when the USSR collapsed, the people in the arms industry no longer enjoyed special care, were now on hard times, and that makes for a dangerous situation.

"With your permission, my friend and I would like to investigate the matter. Through old contacts, we may be able to gather information about the 210 or dispel the information as pure gossip. It would require going into Russia or the old block countries and that is always a concern."

The waiter returned with their drinks, so Rene changed the conversation to the subject of flowers and how he was in the process of writing a book about the history of tulips. "Yes, I am here doing research. Did you know the tulip originally came from Turkey and it is still their national flower?"

"No, I didn't," Gil replied.

Rene continued as the waiter served the two martinis then moved onto other customers.

"Do you know if any Intel organizations are looking into the matter?" Gil inquired when he was sure the waiter was out of earshot.

"No," Rene replied. "The only thing we have is the information from the source."

"That's a little thin," Dunn replied. "I realize he is your friend, but getting information from a source we know nothing about? I don't think so."

"Maybe if I write a name on this cocktail napkin you will reconsider," Rene said, as he removed a felt tip pen from his inside pocket, wrote the name Boris on his napkin, and slid it over so Gil could read it.

"Is that who I think it is?" Dunn inquired.

"Yes," Rene confirmed, as he slid the napkin back in front of him and allowed some condensation from his glass to drop onto the name. As the liquid mixed with the paper, the name became blurred then turned into a blob of unreadable black.

"He was a pain in my ass back in the old days," Gil admitted.

"And mine," Rene added, as both men reflected back to the cold war years.

"That makes things a little different," Gil finally agreed. "We'll meet again before I go back to the States and discuss the details, but for now, it's catch up time," he declared, taking the first sip of his drink.

CHAPTER 2

JJ and Mac stopped to light up two cigars before continuing their walk around the bed and breakfast that was actually home base or The Barn for the Team.

After taking a long drag on his cigar, then exhaling, JJ said, "Time has been going by so quickly. I failed to realize five years had passed since I got you all involved in this fight. Was thinking it may be a good idea to meet with the Team and Board and discuss the matter."

"I agree," Mac acknowledged. "Since we have been at it for so long, it would be a good idea to check with everyone about how they feel about everything and how long they plan to stay on."

"I have written down our T/O and some thoughts I would like you to review when we get back to the house, then we can discuss any questions or concerns you may have," JJ informed Mac.

"Sounds like a plan," Mac replied, as he stopped to light up his cigar again.

Their walk completed, the two men returned to the house that was adjacent to the renovated Barn and proceeded to JJ's den.

"Has your wife ever wondered in the last five years why you two haven't been to the summer house?" Mac inquired.

"Told her four years ago I sold it when we bought the one in Connecticut."

"It's good to be rich," General Mac observed, as the two men entered the den.

"Not that rich," JJ defended.

"Don't give me that shit," Mac replied. "You and the Board could probably throw your loose change into a pot and buy Guam."

JJ just shook his head and smiled as he approached his desk, removed a binder from the top drawer, handed it to Mac, and said, "I realize the Board and Team met during and after the last Project, but I feel you and I should still be the go between for Team and Board."

"Makes sense," Mac agreed, "especially for security considerations."

"I'm going to the kitchen to get a brew, would you like something?" JJ inquired, as he moved toward the door.

"A scotch would be nice," Mac requested, as he sat in one of the chairs in front of the desk.

"Scotch it is."

As JJ left the room, Mac opened the binder, started reviewing the document, and then started down the list of names and JJ's comments.

The Board: JJ, in for the duration. General Mac, still a pain in the ass and probably in for the duration. Gil Dunn, President of

Van Corcoven Firearms Company and former DDO at CIA, will probably stay. Charles Wilson, President of Wilson Explosives Company, will probably stay. Jeff Dawson, President of International Oil, still seems eager to be involved. John Howard, President of Zerk Pharmaceutical, may be starting to wane a little. Admiral Fox (Foxie), Mac this one is your call.

Team total eleven listed by code name: I feel most will stay; they seem to have become family. Have flagged a few of the Team due to business concerns. They have been away from their ongoing businesses a lot during the past five years and may want to return to them full time.

Team Leader, JC, retired Marine Corps Colonel, pilot, expert with weapons, and our main gizmo man. Has stated would stay as long he felt the Team was needed in the war on terrorism.

Blue Jay, Field Team Leader, contract type, prior to that, Marine Corps and CIA.

Bean, part-time contractor type, prior Army Airborne Ranger, Special Forces, and CIA.

Benz, Japanese, expert in martial arts, been in the contract business for many years.

Panda, Philippino, also martial arts, takes on contracts from time to time, regular occupation: engineering consultant.

Check, Arab, explosives, takes on contracts from time to time, owns a Middle East restaurant. May have business concerns?

Tic, Cuban, explosives, also part-timer, regular occupation: stockbroker. May have business concerns?

Bris, French, primarily a contractor, but also an artist and a good one.

Pru, English, contractor, long-range shooter.

Met, German, also a contractor, long-range shooter.

Air Jockey, contractor, can fly helicopters, most prop aircraft, the corporate jet, and able to function as a Team member on the ground if needed.

House Team: Top Kiner, retired 1st Sgt. Marine Corps. Lady1 and LadyA, former Intelligence operatives. The three have become unplanned assets in the fight. In addition to maintaining home base, they have been active participants in several Projects.

Also looking for your thoughts on this next topic.

As you know, we brought three former CIA operatives and their wives to this area due to the Al-Qaeda attempted kidnapping and probable assassination a while back. Should we just keep them close for their own safety or ask them if they want to get involved with our Projects?

Mac had just finished reading when JJ returned with two scotch and waters.

"This brings up a lot of what ifs," Mac said, as he accepted his drink. "If one of the Board members decides to drop out, it would mean a big hit on the financial support. If two drop out, it will probably be the ball game. As for the Team, we can't really afford to lose any. We may be able to limp along if one or two departed, but more than two and we'll be folding our tents. As for the House Team, I feel they will stay on for the duration if they can get into the field from time to time."

"I know," JJ agreed. "I'm just starting to get used to letting the Ladies go out on Projects."

"As for the three former CIA operatives, I think we should sit down with Gil Dunn, Blue Jay, and Bean to get their input. They all worked for Gil at CIA and Jar Head, Doggie, and Swabbie recruited and trained Blue Jay and Bean."

"Good idea," JJ agreed, "and if we all agree with bringing them onboard, they would have a better idea of where the three would best fit in."

SOT 4 – Trail of the Isotopes

JJ and Mac continued reviewing and discussing the document, then decided the most logical chain of events would be to first call a meeting and ask the Board. Without financial support, the Projects would end. If everything went well with the Board, the Team and House Team would be next followed by a meeting with Dunn, Blue Jay, and Bean about the former CIA operatives.

CHAPTER 3

With everyone on the Board and Teams agreeing to stay for at least another year or as General Mac put it, 'Shipped over for another tour', the Board was again in a planning session. As in the past, three Projects would be discussed, a vote taken, and the Project getting the most votes would be passed onto the Team for final approval.

Presentation and discussion for two possible Projects had just been completed and JJ was again calling the meeting to order for the third time.

"Gentleman," JJ started, getting everyone's attention. "The third Project is a little out of the norm for our usual mode of operation and much more complex. Usually, the Team has an objective and plan for their insertion, extraction, and performing of the task. This Project would involve the Team sort of acting as a security force for the people sent to do the deed." JJ paused, as he looked at the wondering faces of the Board. "It gets better."

He continued. "The people sent to do the deed would be unaware of the Team's involvement."

"Okay! I'll ask it," Mr. Wilson chimed in. "Where in the fuck did you get this one?"

"Don't kill the messenger," JJ defended. "This actually came from a new addition to our group and once we get into the details, you will realize it's not as hard as it initially sounded, it's harder," JJ advised. "I could try to present this, but know more questions would be asked than I could answer and that would lead to more meetings. I felt the best way to proceed would be to let the original source present it. Bringing new people here would bring attention to this location and the Barn is not a good idea for the same reason, so Mac and I thought my cabin in Pennsylvania would be a good idea. Swabbie, Jar Head, Doggie, and their wives are temporarily in residence and the Team would handle all security for your transportation to the location."

"You all remember the cabin, don't you?" Mac inquired.

"That's where we all went for small arms training. Wilson killed all of the weeds with his Thompson submachine gun and became know as The Weed Whacker."

"Better than being known as General Tallywhacker," Wilson immediately replied.

Mac knew he wouldn't have to wait long for a reply and immediately burst into laughter followed by Wilson and the other Board members.

"I'm glad you mentioned that, Mac," JJ spoke up. "After we finish up with this topic, I want to discuss the involvement of the Board members in the last two Projects. For many reasons, it is not a good idea for members to be on the front lines in this war and we are lucky we all survived."

"We all survived because we didn't get in front of The Weedwhacker," Mac instigated.

"Is that why you survived, Tally?" Wilson snapped.

JJ knew where things were heading and wisely called for a coffee break before they discussed arrangements for the trip to the cabin or him expressing concerns about the Board getting too close to the action. He already knew with this group his concerns would probably go into one ear and out the other, but it would make him feel better.

———————

Two days had passed since the Board's last meeting and Dawson was the last Board member to arrive at a county park about fifteen miles from the cabin. After leaving his car in a parking lot, he followed a walking trail that worked its way through the park. As he approached another parking area, he noticed a dark suburban with shaded windows, approached it, opened the back door, and got in joining the other Board members.

"Mr. Brown, I believe," the driver announced, as Dawson sat back against the seat.

"Hello, Bris," Mr. Dawson replied. "How have you been?"

"Can't complain," Bris replied, as he turned the key in the ignition and the engine in the suburban came to life.

JJ and Mac had originally assigned code names to all of the Team members when it was formed. JJ had to do the same for the Board, under rather hasty conditions, and decided on colors as code names.

"Are we clear?" Bris inquired into his com unit.

"You're clear," were several replies from other Team members handling security in the area of the foot trail and parked cars. Some of the Team members on security detail would secure the cars in the parking lot while others in cars would handle security to and from the cabin.

After getting the clear signal, Bris eased the suburban to the entrance of the parking lot, paused, and then turned left, headed toward the park exit, and the drive to the cabin. With Bris initiating conversations about the weather, sports, and other topics, it made the travel time pass quickly and in no time, they were close to the lane that led to the cabin.

"Anything interesting up there?" Bris inquired into his com unit.

"Not much of anything," was the reply from Benz and Panda, as their Audi passed the lane about a quarter of a mile ahead of the suburban.

"How about back there?" Bris then inquired to Check and Tic in the BMW about a quarter of a mile behind.

"Very quiet road," came the confirmation that the road was clear.

In a matter of seconds, the suburban had made the turn onto the lane and disappeared into the woods as it rounded the first of a few curves on the way to the cabin.

The Audi and BMW would not proceed to the cabin, but would wait in the immediate area until they were notified about the return trip.

When the suburban came to a stop in front of the cabin, JJ and Mac were there to greet the board members and escort them into the cabin.

After reintroductions to Swabbie, Jar Head, Doggie, and their wives, the Board members were seated in a makeshift briefing area. After the wives excused themselves and went outside to harass Bris and any other Team members they could find, JJ brought the briefing to order. "As I stated at our last meeting," JJ started, "thought it better if these three men were present at this meeting and since Swabbie received the information firsthand, he should conduct the briefing. That said,

I'll turn it over to you," JJ said, as he gestured toward Swabbie who was already standing next to an easel at the other end of the room.

"Let me first warn you all that in the past, I have been accused of being a detailed briefer," Swabbie started.

"Amen to that," Gil immediately agreed with a smile.

"I received the information I am about to relay to you from a man we will call The Latino." Swabbie continued. "But first let me give you some background on him.

"Jar Head, Doggie, and I became acquainted with him back in the early seventies when he was a Cuban operative in Nicaragua and we were trying to eliminate him. Long story short, accompanied by a local four-man kill squad, we were sent to the island of Cayos to hunt him down. We found where he was living, he was not there, but his wife and two young sons were, and the kill squad wanted to terminate the family. We objected, they threatened us, gunfire erupted, and they went for a dirt nap.

"Now I'm going to fast forward about twenty years to nineteen ninety-three. We were having a little problem in the Intel community and one night after parking my car, I was walking to a restaurant in DC when The Latino and his two grown sons popped out of nowhere. At that point in time, I had never met the man, but he put me at ease with the story about Cayos and how we saved his family. After telling him I remembered the incident, he told me he wanted to repay us. I tried to assure him there was no need, but he said it was a matter of honor and solved a big problem we were having in the Intel community. Gil was DDO at the time and can verify what I'm telling you." Swabbie paused, giving Dunn a chance to speak.

"Yes, I remember," Gil confirmed. "If memory serves, he also helped save Doggie and Jar Heads' lives."

"And the good side of that was…" Swabbie inquired to Gil. "Sorry, sorry," Swabbie quickly apologized. "Up here giving a briefing I must have had a flashback to the old days."

"Nancy had a flashback," Doggie alerted Jar Head.

"Yeah, how about that. It must have been during the time when he went into pussy management back in DC while we stayed in the field and fought evil."

"Now I'm having flashbacks and the three reasons I retired from the DDO business," Gil said as everyone broke into laughter.

When the laughter subsided, Swabbie continued the briefing. "Now that you know a little about the source, I'll get to the heart of the matter. I understand for security reasons it is a Board policy to assign code names to individuals in your Projects in an effort to prevent accidental disclosure. If an accidental disclosure happened and it is a code name, no one would know the real name of the person, so we'll call our bad guy Big Face.

"As you all know, Castro is the linchpin that keeps Cuba together. Since he is seriously ill, Raul had been given power, on a temporary basis, but only because he is Castro's brother, not because he is a good leader. Raul has a history of being weak that dates back to the days of the revolution when even the common man and woman in Cuba knew it.

"Since there have been riots in Cuba that in some cases required the appearance of Castro to quell the rioters, some analysts feel when Castro dies, no one else in Cuba would be strong enough to keep the current communist government in power. There will be many upheavals and the country would revert to a capitalist society followed by Cuba – US relations being restored. This is probably a good analysis if all outside interests keep a hands-off policy, but we all know that isn't going to happen especially with Big Face making so many visits to Cuba.

"At this point in time, Castro probably realizes his days are numbered. No one in Cuba is strong enough to keep the government together and is trying to find a way to get Big Face involved to keep communism as the main power in Cuba at any cost. Castro has been a diehard communist since the beginning, but due to his age or being in power too long, had forgotten one thing: the Cuban people. They may be poor, but they are proud and would not be willing to allow a foreign power, especially a Hispanic foreign power, to have control in their country. Warned you, I was a detailed briefer, but we're at the main point of the presentation," Swabbie said, as he paused for a sip of water.

"No problem," Jar Head encouraged followed by, "wake up, Doggie, we're at the main point."

"Already?" Doggie asked, as he faked a yawn and stretched his arms.

"Now I'm having flashbacks of the two main reasons I retired," Swabbie informed the group who again chuckled.

"Our source, The Latino, was disgusted with the communist regimen back in ninety-three and took his family into exile, but maintained some of his sources in the Caribbean and South American Intelligence communities and is privy to some very sensitive information about a complex plan to help ensure Big Face gets a foothold in Cuba.

"From this point on, it gets involved so I'll do it by the numbers. One, a group in Miami plans to assassinate Raul after Castro's death. Two, that group has been infiltrated by foreign Intel and knows their every move. Three, Big Face plans to allow the assassination of Raul, then ambush the assassins on the spot, and turn them over to the Cuban government for a public trial pointing out how it was a US plot. Four, Big Face becomes a hero and the power behind the throne. Since he has already cultivated the next person in succession behind Raul and confirmed that allegiance with huge sums of money, he sees a win-win for himself.

"I realize compared to the first part of the briefing this was quick and to the point, but am sure if I hadn't gone into such detail, your first questions would have been about the source."

"About the source," Mac inquired, "why did he contact you with this information?"

"He didn't want to just dump this information and let it find its way up the chain to the top, so I was the logical choice. He figured I probably still had contacts inside the Intelligence community, plus we have a history."

"Cuba can be a big place if you have to be in position at a certain time with very short notice. Will The Latino be supplying you with that information?" Mac again inquired.

"He will be staying in close touch with his source in Miami and will relay the plan to me ASAP," Swabbie answered.

"I also have two questions," JJ spoke up. "One, what does he expect from the Intelligence community? And two, did he make any recommendations on how to resolve the situation?"

"The answers are, he didn't say and no. I'm guessing you have concerns about a setup?" Swabbie inquired and JJ shook his head yes. "As we all know, anything is possible. People change, allegiances change. It could be a setup and even if the information is true, it would be so high level and sensitive it would be almost impossible to verify. But if it is true and no one acts, we could have Big Face sitting on our doorstep planning who knows what and the Cuban people not too happy with the US."

"History does repeat itself," Dunn said aloud. "I remember a situation back when Anwar Saddat was president of Egypt and they were friends with Russia. What Saddat didn't know was his vice president had been recruited by the KGB. Saddat's assassination was in the planning stages and that would have given the Soviet Union a strong foothold in the Middle East. Unfortunately for them, the Agency uncovered the plot, presented the proof to Saddat, the VP went to prison, and Egypt became more friendly with the US. It is obvious that can't be done this time, especially with the information coming from the US, so if anything, some sort of elaborate plan would have to be undertaken to get a similar result."

After a pause, Swabbie inquired, "Are there any other questions?" When no one spoke up, he ended the presentation with a question of his own. "The Hispanic gave me this information to forward onto the Intelligence community. Should I do that or would you all like some time to think about it?"

"Time seems to be a problem in more ways than one," JJ spoke up. "The attempted assassination will not take place until after Castor's death. How long after is unknown. Would we have enough time to plan and prepare? In addition to that, we have the verification of the information problem."

"It is hairy," Dunn agreed, "but we may be able to verify bits and pieces of the information. Especially since huge sums of finances were supposedly given to Raul's successor. If we could locate a money trail, it would verify that part of the puzzle."

"It would probably be next to impossible to verify anything on the other end, but could we verify the original plan to assassinate Raul?" Mr. Howard inquired.

"That may be doable," Dunn answered. "There are always rumors afloat, it's just figuring out which ones are true and which are just rumors."

"That is very true," Foxie made his entry, "but if the information is correct, the plan may be to control Cuba, embarrass the US, and to also bring pressure for us to give up the naval base at Gtmo. They have been trying to get us out of there for years and with Big Face working behind the scenes, he would really want us out of the area."

"These are all valid points, so let's revisit the time issue," JJ again spoke. "If we are not going to act on this information, we should waste no time in passing it onto US Intel. If we do take it on, we should waste no time in starting Project planning with the condition if the information verification hits a snag or a gray area, we immediately turn it over to US Intel along with our findings. I'm sure Gil could find a creditable source at CIA."

That's scary, Gil thought to himself. *I was thinking Di Flippi would be an excellent choice.*

"So you're calling for a vote?" Dawson inquired.

"Yes, I think it may be a good idea," JJ confirmed, "unless someone objects."

All of the Board members agreed a vote was in order; it was taken and was unanimous.

After the vote was taken, JJ again had the floor. "Since we are all in agreement, the Team should be briefed as soon as possible so we can get a yes or no from them. Swabbie, could you do that tomorrow at the Barn?"

"No problem," Swabbie assured JJ.

"Good," JJ answered. "We'll make arrangements to have you all transported to the Barn early tomorrow morning. While you, Jar Head, and Doggie are at the briefing, the ladies can get reacquainted with LadyA, Lady1, and Top at the main house."

"Sounds like a plan," Swabbie assured him.

"Well, I guess that will do it for this session," JJ said, ending the meeting.

"Our wives have prepared some refreshments if you would like to have some," Jar Head suggested.

"They do make killer cakes and pies," Doggie volunteered, "but we'll understand if you can't stay. It would be very difficult for the three of us, but I'm sure we could force ourselves to eat all of the goodies."

"Now we can't allow you to force yourselves to do something like that," Wilson said, as he stood and inquired about the location of the cakes.

"It's only fair we help them out, "Mac agreed, as he stood and inquired about the pies.

"Good," Swabbie said and went outside to inform the ladies that everyone would be staying for refreshments.

Swabbie had presented the briefing to the Team and just completed relaying the decisions, concerns, and suggestions from the Board's briefing the day before.

"That completes the briefing," Swabbie informed the Team. "Are there any questions?"

"I have to echo JJ's concerns about the time issue," JC spoke up. "I understand we will be updated by The Hispanic on the plan in Miami. However, the amount of time between when they decide to execute the plan and our finding out about it concerns me. We could develop a Project and be ready to go, but must have time to get into place."

"The time element could be eliminated if we could get pre-positioned in Cuba, but again, we need to know the location of the assassination attempt," Blue Jay added.

"Getting in and out of Cuba will be another problem," Air Jockey spoke up. "The last time we didn't have much trouble getting in, but getting out was fun."

When Jockey finished, the remainder of the Team fired off questions and concerns almost faster than Swabbie could handle them. "I know the Team will vote on the Project," Swabbie finally acknowledged, "and with all of these rapid-fire questions right off the bat, I can guess what that vote will be. Maybe I should just turn it over to the Intelligence community?"

"Now don't be too hasty," Blue Jay recommended.

"Yeah, we're just clearing our palates," JC confirmed.

"Does this bring back any memories?" Jar Head whispered to Doggie.

"Yes, it does," he replied, "and we were the ones asking the questions. Knew I liked this group."

"Me, too," Jar Head agreed.

JJ and Mac were enjoying the roles as spectators at this briefing. They were usually the ones up there fielding the rapid-fire questions from the Team. JJ almost intervened once when it looked like they had Swabbie on the ropes, but Jar Head and Doggie got into the mix and they were all off and running again.

This was the norm when presenting a new Project. The Team would beat the shit out of the presenters with questions and personal observations.

About one hour later, Swabbie again asked, "Are there any other questions?"

When no one spoke up, he looked at JJ and inquired, "I guess it's onto the next phase?"

"Your guess is correct," JJ confirmed, as he stood up to address the group. "The Team will have meetings to discuss the Project, and then will vote in a day or so. If there are no other questions, we'll adjourn to the house for lunch."

"I'd like to have a word with the Team first," JC spoke up. "Could you give our visitors a tour of the Barn while we meet?"

"Sure," JJ assured, as Mac and he escorted the three men toward the door.

The tour was in the Como Shack looking at some of JC's gizmos when Bean appeared in the doorway. "We're ready to reconvene," he informed everyone.

After the tour returned and had taken their seats, JC started to speak. "I realize this is out of the norm, but there is a reason," JC started. "I am afraid at this point in time the best you're going to get is a tentative yes vote. For one reason, there are too many unknowns.

"However, we also feel Project planning should start right away in case the unknowns work themselves out. To save time, we could departmentalize the planning with Mac monitoring all processes. When the plan is completed, we can present each element to the Team as a whole.

"The reason I'm bringing this up now is we feel new blood and different ideas might be in order and suggest if they are willing, Swabbie, Jar Head, and Doggie join us in the planning stage."

Blue Jay saw the surprised trio was at a loss for words so he added, "Bean and I abstained from the voting due to our relationship with you three. JC suggested it and they voted unanimously in favor."

When Swabbie regained his composure, he quickly communicated with the other two men, then spoke. "It would be our privilege."

"Oh, good," a voice in the crowd spoke out. "I guess this one will be The Quad Floating Simplicity," referring to the name JC had given to a rescue Project that was very hastily planned.

"Spare me," Mac added. "I just started sleeping again since the last time I was reminded about The Floating Simplicity."

"You'll get used to that," JC assured the trio, as they looked back at the others.

"Knew I liked this group," Doggie said aloud.

"It'll be like the old days," Jar Head agreed.

Bean and Blue Jay looked at each other, then looked at JC, and asked in unison, "Can we take a leave of absence?"

"What do you mean a leave of absence?" Doggie inquired. "It will be like the old days, you'll like it."

"Yeah, it will be like déjà vu all over again," Jar Head assured them. "You two and your adopted dads."

"Maybe we should just go over the hill," Bean told Blue Jay. "It isn't like this is the military and we would be breaking the law."

"I have an idea," Blue Jay offered, as everyone started moving toward the door. "We'll put a sticky note on the kitchen door after lunch then run like hell."

"Good idea," Bean agreed. "Fuck this and goodbye, Your friends B and BJ."

"Wait a minute, why do you have top billing?" Blue Jay inquired. "Why can't the note read BJ and B."

"Because I composed the note, dickhead!" Bean replied, as they passed through the doorway.

"Going over the hill might be a good idea," Swabbie informed Mac and JJ as they all stood.

The two men started laughing and assured Swabbie they would all have a lot to share over lunch.

———————

When the men arrived at the house, they were informed they would be having lunch in the dining room. The women were still catching up and would be lunching in the kitchen.

There was a lot of conversation during lunch in both the kitchen and dining room. The women had a chance to get acquainted during the ride back from Virginia after the House Team quelled an Al-Qaeda kidnapping, assassination attempt, but hadn't had anytime to talk since.

When things started to quiet down in the dining room, Top inquired, "Everyone ready for dessert?" and got a unanimous, "Yes."

Top stood up and left for the kitchen then returned a minute later.

"Think I'll give the Ladies a few more minutes. They're a little upset," he told the others.

"Is something wrong?" Jar Head inquired, thinking Top was including the wives in his statement.

"No, no, I was referring to Lady1 and LadyA," Top assured him then added, "I am surprised they are sharing that information though."

"Are you kidding, those three could get water out of a stone," Doggie informed him.

"Well, since they are sharing with the women, I guess I can fill you in a little," Top volunteered. "Years back, LadyA and Lady1 were married to two military types that I served with and that's how I came to know both of them. At that time, one of the ladies worked for CIA, the other DIA, and both were field operatives. After their husbands were killed in the line of duty, they threw themselves totally into their work and never really got into a serious relationship ever again."

JJ and Mac were already aware of what Top was saying, but the Team was surprised and a little saddened.

After a few seconds of quiet, Bean inquired, "So you figured you would give them some time to regroup in the kitchen?"

"That, plus I like the way all of my body parts work," Top answered.

"Well, I'm not afraid," Bean assured him, as he stood up tall, went to the doorway, and yelled down the hall to the kitchen, "Wench, the dessert!" After delivering his message, Bean bent over and scurried back to his seat as everyone commented on what was probably going to happen next.

There was total silence in the kitchen for a few seconds after the message arrived, then, "Wench, the dessert is it, I'll give him dessert," LadyA said, as she stood up and walked over to the refrigerator, opened the door, and removed a chocolate meringue pie.

The three wives looked at Lady1 who said, "It isn't going to be pretty."

As LadyA walked into the dining room, it sounded like stampeding cattle came down the hall and stopped on a dime. A few seconds later, the other women strolled nonchalantly into the room each caring a dessert.

"Did someone request dessert?" LadyA inquired, as she moved down Bean's side of the table. "Was it you, Panda?" she inquired, as she passed behind his chair.

"It was not I, Lady," Panda answered, as the suspense grew.

"He's going to get a face full of pie," Met whispered.

"Give you two to one odds he doesn't," Mrs. Doggie whispered a wager.

"For twenty," Met inquired and she shook her head in agreement.

"I say, I'd like some of that action," Pru said very quietly.

"You're on," Mrs. Jar Head whispered in his ear.

Everyone was getting in on the action as LadyA asked, "Was it you, Jockey?"

"It was not I, Lady," Jockey also answered.

LadyA then stopped behind Bean, put her right hand on his right shoulder, and asked, "Was it you, Bean?"

"I cannot tell a lie," Bean confessed, then said, "It was him," as he pointed at Blue Jay across the table.

On that note, LadyA's right hand grabbed under Bean's jaw and pulled his head back so he was facing the ceiling, put her left foot on his left leg, and said, "You're the one that called for the Desert Wench" she declared, then planted a big kiss on his lips. "Will it be pie or thigh?" she then inquired.

"Can I have pie after thigh?" he asked in a pleading, timid voice.

LadyA couldn't keep a straight face after hearing the reply and said, "You asshole," then started to laugh and was joined by everyone else at the table.

As everyone continued laughing and commenting about the incident, the women were collecting their bets. "Come on, cough it up," Mrs. Jar Head badgered Pru.

"I say, it's getting rather expensive to eat here," he declared, as he paid the twenty dollars.

CHAPTER 4

After all of the unknown factors were cleared up, planning went into high gear at the Barn. All of the plan elements were presented, a final product was approved, and the Team was ready to go.

"Are you taking Uncle Fudd for his flying lesson today?" Panda inquired, as he walked past JC and Mac who were looking at a map.

"I'll give you Uncle Fudd, you peckerhead!" Mac fired back.

"Now don't get Fudd all upset," Air Jockey reprimanded Panda. "You know how old people are."

"Why am I not surprised the pilot from Pussy Airways is in the area and also has something to say," Mac observed. "Birds of the feather, only in this case, shit birds of the feather." Then he added, "You children be careful, don't want you tripping and skinning your knee."

Panda and Jockey burst into laughter as they continued on their way.

JC and Mac were flying in a seaplane at 4,000 feet when Mac said, "A lot of water down there."

"You find that is usually true when you're flying over seas and oceans!" JC quipped.

Mac just looked at JC then out the front window and said, "If you get any closer, you're going to give that rudder a haircut."

"I want to make damn sure we are showing up on Cuban radar as one blip," JC replied, as he put a little more distance between them and the Team's plane ahead of them.

"It's almost time for my flying lesson," Mac said, as he looked at his watch. "Shall I turn on the radio for everyone's listening enjoyment?"

"We probably should get in a little chatter before the main event," JC acknowledged.

Mac turned on the plane's radio, then motioned for JC to start the conversation.

"Okay, I realize this is only your second lesson, but just relax when you take the controls. Understand?" JC asked.

"Yeah," was the nervous reply.

Air Jockey alerted the Team they were about to perform a planned maneuver. "We're on."

"We will do this by the numbers. On the count of three, you will take the controls, okay?" JC inquired to his make-believe student.

"Yeah," was another nervous reply.

"Boy, Mac has a big part in this play," Panda observed and the Team chuckled.

"I'll start counting slowly and when I get to three, you will have control. One, two, three."

On the count of three, both JC and Jockey put their aircrafts into the same angle dive they had practiced so many times in the past week.

As both planes headed for the sea below, JC started his chatter. "Pull up!" was his first instruction followed by, "I said pull up!" A more anxious command as the plane disappeared off Cuban radar.

Knowing their blip just went off the scope, JC pulled his craft out of its dive while Jockey continued even lower before leveling off at almost wave top level.

As JC and Mac once again appeared on Cuban radar, JC's voice could again be heard on the radio. "What the fuck was that about? You almost put us into the water."

After attempting to give control to his student a few more times with similar results, the frustrated instructor, after more outbursts on the radio, called it a day and turned back toward the Bahamas.

"Thus ends another episode of Will they go for the ruse," Bean said aloud, as their plane headed for their destination on the Cuban shore.

"I'm sort of hoping the Cubans didn't get that much needed repair done on that radar station and still can't scan below three hundred feet," Jockey remarked, as he tried to keep the plane around 100 feet.

Since Castro's death, Raul had been very pressed with just trying to keep on top of fast moving events and was convinced to take a brief retreat away from all of the every day stress. Due to its calm and scenic beauty, a remote villa along the coast not far from Marea del Portillo on the southeast coast of Cuba was suggested and Raul gave his okay for the retreat location. From that point on, the race was on. The different sources reported the information about the retreat location and three groups were put into motion. The Team was one of the groups and had the most challenging tasks. They had to get into that area of Cuba and be in position first in order to execute their elaborate plans.

———— ———— ————

The sun had set and a dull gray had set in over the Caribbean Sea just before total darkness would engulf the entire area. Jockey had on his night vision gear, but was hoping he would not have to land the seaplane in total darkness.

"According to the GPS, we are at touchdown," Blue Jay reported from the co-pilot's seat.

"Well, here goes nothing," Air Jockey advised, as he eased the plane down onto the water for a landing.

The plane had made a perfect landing and came to a stop just off the shoreline when Blue Jay started to talk into his com unit. "According to this GPS and the coordinates we were given, that hidden cove should be in the immediate area."

The two men in the cockpit were scanning the shoreline with their night vision gear looking for the entrance to the cove when Jockey said, "The only thing I can see is something that looks a little out of the norm over there to the left."

Blue Jay immediately looked to the same area, agreed, and with no other options available, Jockey started to taxi the plane in that direction. As they got close to the area in question, it seemed either the GPS or the coordinates were wrong. The cliff face along the shore followed the shoreline then it seemed to make an abrupt left turn toward the sea. As the plane approached the left turn in the cliff, Jockey throttled back the plane and guided it to the right. As its forward motion came to a stop, Jockey exclaimed, "I'll be dammed, talk about a hidden cove. Who knew about this spot?"

Blue Jay didn't say anything but knew when Foxie was commanding officer at Gtmo, he had Seal Teams running recon missions into Cuba and had probably used this hidden cove as an entry point for this part of the island.

Jockey eased the throttles forward and the plane moved toward the entrance of the cove. The opening didn't give much room for error, but Jockey managed to navigate the plane inside then headed slowly toward the beach.

Benz had the side door of the plane open, was testing the depth with a weighted line, and reported it over the com unit. Some of these coves drop off real quick not far from the beach and it just wouldn't do for the first man out the door to just disappear.

Benz reported, "Four feet!" Jockey cut the engines and let the plane coast to a stop.

After making a quick check around the inside of the cove, Blue Jay ordered, "Let's do it," and Benz eased into the water with weapon at the ready followed by Check with his MP5 in one hand and a rope to secure the plane to the shore in the other. Being covered by Team members in the doorway and from the opened window in the cockpit, the two made their way to shore about fifteen feet away. Once ashore, they secured the line to a big palm tree, disappeared from the beach, and performed a quick recon. Within a few minutes, the Duo was back on the beach and signaled the others to come ashore and perform a more detailed reconnaissance of the area.

With the area secured, the Team set to the task of concealing their ride home. The primary concern was being seen by a low flying aircraft, so great detail was given to the overhead. If someone actually entered the small cove, no amount of camouflage could conceal the seaplane that was floating just offshore. After they were satisfied with the overhead camouflage, they waited a few more hours in case they were seen and the Cuban military were on the way. Air Jockey and Tic monitored Cuban military radio traffic as the Team again went over the details of the plan.

The Team would split into two units. Bean would lead one unit with Benz and Panda, and Bris would continue up the shoreline and set up at a location where the group from Miami was supposed to come ashore. Blue Jay, Tic, Met, and Pru would turn inland toward the villa where Raul was enjoying his holiday.

"Think we've covered everything unless I've overlooked something..." Blue Jay questioned, as he looked at the other Team members.

When no one responded, he said, "Weapons and night vision gear, check." Everyone rechecked their MP5 and Beretta 9mm sidearm. In addition to those weapons, Pru and Met would each carry a Russian SV-98 sniper rifle.

"Rubber gloves?" Blue Jay inquired to Met and Pru who both held their hands in the air revealing the rubber gloves they were wearing then returned to wiping the SV-98 clean of any unwanted fingerprints.

Satisfied that the two units were ready to move out, Blue Jay huddled with Air Jockey and Check. "With any luck you will not be discovered. I realize you know what to do, but want to emphasize there is no need for heroics. Just burn the plane and proceed to the coordinates I gave you. We'll all rendezvous there and go into the mountains until things quiet down, then we'll execute the extraction we developed during the planning stage. Okay?" he inquired and both men shook their heads in agreement.

The Team members were moving and jumping around checking their gear for any noises when Jockey wandered over by Panda. "Getting any better with that MP-5, dickhead?"

"If you weren't the only pilot on this trip I'd show you," Panda fired back.

"Good thing it's an automatic weapon, especially in your case." Jockey continued pretending he didn't hear Panda's remark.

"You just make sure the ride's here for the return trip," Panda ordered then added, "Don't get bored and take the plane for a joyride over Havana, asshole."

"What's the matter, Mac's not here so you have to pick on each other?" Bean inquired.

"Yeah, he's never around when you need him," Jockey agreed then said, "Be careful," as his hand pushed against Panda's shoulder.

The Team always got a chuckle out of these two. If they weren't teamed up and stirring up something, they were picking on each other.

Satisfied everyone was ready, Blue Jay first performed a check with the radios Bean and Jockey had, then a Team check to make sure everyone could send and receive over the com units. That done, he said, "Let's move out," and the Team moved off the beach.

After traveling about two miles up the coast, the group came to a halt. "This is the location," Blue Jay said softly into his com unit. "Let's check out the area."

As the Team members performed a detailed recon of the area, Blue Jay told Bean the same thing he told Jockey and Check. "No heroics," Blue Jay ordered, "you know what I'm saying. If it gets too hot, back off. The worst thing that could happen is an extended tour in the scenic Cuban mountains."

"Okay," Bean agreed with a smile.

Satisfied the area was secured, positioning and camouflage for the four-man unit were started, and with the help of the other Team members, the unit started blending into the landscape until they became invisible.

"Looks good," Blue Jay approved, as his unit stood back and admired the Team's handiwork. "We're going to move out," Blue Jay advised. "Good luck and see you all at the rendezvous." The other members of the Team wished each other luck, as the other unit moved onto their location around the villa.

Once Blue Jay's unit cleared the immediate area, he picked up the pace. Getting to this location first was very important, but getting to the area around the villa first was imperative.

The unit covered the three miles to the villa in about fifty minutes, then moved very slow and deliberate until Blue Jay signaled to halt into his com unit. "Let's hold up here and check it out," he ordered and each man removed a pair of small but powerful field glasses from their inside pockets and started viewing the area from left to right and back again. Each time they completed a scan, they positioned the glasses a little higher and scanned again until each man had scanned from very close to their area to the villa itself. With no suspicious activity reported, each man then returned to things in the area that deserved a second look.

Not seeing anything out of the ordinary, the four men melted into the landscape and waited. While they kept the area under surveillance, Blue Jay thought to himself, *If these Projects get any more complex, we are all going to need cue cards. The people from Miami want to assassinate Raul, the people from Big Face land know the plan and want to capture or kill the Miami people after the assassination. That would eliminate Raul and put Big Face's man into power, make BF a hero to the Cuban people,*

*and allow him to point the finger at the US and drive a big wedge
between the two. So all we have to do is be in the middle and
make changes to the script. Glad I'm working with these people.
With a Team of lesser quality could spell disaster trying to pull
off a stunt like this.*

The night was uneventful, but as night started giving way to
day, Pru's voice came over on the com unit. "I say, I believe we
have some chaps in camouflage at two o'clock." All eyes turned
in that direction.

"I count six," Met added after a brief pause.

The unit just observed the six men and allowed them to take
up positions for the ambush that would occur just after Raul's
assassination. Setting up in the right place for the ambush was a
best guess situation, but the leader seemed to know his stuff and
after surveying the area, he decided to position his men in an area
just behind the best guess location. Unfortunately, for them that
location was about twenty yards in front of Blue Jay's unit.

Once the leader was satisfied with everyone's placement,
they settled in and waited for the people from Miami.

———————

Bean and his unit were also waiting for the group from Miami
and he was starting to wonder if they had the right place when he
noticed movement to his left front and immediately alerted his
unit. "Count five," Bris said very softly into his com unit.

This could be a Cuban patrol or maybe another team that will
be in place to intercept anyone that escaped the ambush.

As Bean observed the men, he spoke into the radio. "Are you
on?"

A surprised look came over Blue Jay's face when he heard
Bean's voice in his left ear. If Blue Jay talked into the radio, it

would give away their positions, so instead he clicked the button on the radio mike four times signaling Bean he could not respond verbally.

"Understand," Bean replied then proceeded with yes or no questions. "Have men on foot in the area. Will execute the original plan and at the same time engage whoever these new people are. Do you agree?" Bean asked and one click for a yes was heard over the radio.

"If things don't work out, will back off and contact you at the alternate rendezvous point." Bean then waited and one click was heard again. "EOT," Bean said into the mike.

This shit just gets more and more interesting, Blue Jay thought. *This new wrinkle will also require a little modification at my end. The plan was for Bean to discourage the Miami people prior to me executing this part of the plan. Now with those new people in Bean's area, if the people from Miami show up before Raul makes an appearance and Bean has to engage that other group, all hell could break loose on this end. I hate my job!* were Blue Jay's last thoughts, as he focused his field glasses on the villa hoping to catch a glimpse of Raul.

There was no need to alert his unit about the changes at this time. They already knew when he gave the word the six people in front of them would be taken out quickly and very quietly.

The minutes seemed like hours as everyone waited, then Bean was again in Blue Jay's ear. "You on," and four clicks went over the airways. "High speed vessel heading straight for the beach; looks like a drug running boat. They must also know about radar station maintenance problems?" Bean informed him and got a one-click reply.

Blue Jay was now forced to act. If those people that showed up in Bean's area report back as soon as they are engaged, it could fuck up everything. "Okay, people, by the numbers," he whispered into the com. "One, two, three…" and 4 super silenced MP5's whispered a death song for the six-man team in front of them. The instant the MP5's stopped firing, the unit was on their feet and quickly moved to check the downed men. That completed, Blue Jay was again looking through his glasses and talking into the radio. "You on?"

"I'm on," Bean replied.

"Thought it better if I acted first," Blue Jay explained.

"Understood," was the reply.

"You in a bad situation?" he then asked.

"We should be able to deal with it," Bean assured him, "will get back to you later."

"That's a roger," he said, signing off.

After talking on the radio, Blue Jay took up a position next to a large tree where Pru and Met were getting into position with their Russian SV-98 sniper rifles.

Tic was using a range finder to report the distance from their position to a patio behind the huge house when he said, "Hello, a bonus at eleven o'clock."

Blue Jay immediately swung to 11:00 and the vice president's face appeared in his glasses. "Looks like he wants to assume power without delay," Blue Jay commented.

"Maybe we should do something about that," Tic suggested.

"I say, since we have this opportunity, we should take the shot," Pru agreed, as he and Met finished putting rubber gloves on two of the dead men.

"It is tempting," Blue Jay agreed, "but the plan is to breeze a few rounds past Raul's head, plant the rifles on these men, and haul ass."

"Here's Raulie," Tic again reported, as Raul joined the others on the patio.

"Now remember, close, but not too close," Blue Jay ordered then Tic gave the range to target.

"Anytime you're ready," Blue Jay then instructed and both men took up the slack in their trigger squeeze and a few seconds later, two rounds were heading toward the patio.

Raul was so startled when the rounds whistled past his ear that he jumped up out of his seat.

"Good job," Blue Jay commended. "You scared the shit out of him, but he's still breathing."

"Don't think the VP was that lucky," Tic reported into his com unit.

"What!" an astonished Blue Jay inquired, as he verified what was just reported. "Did you misunderstand when I said not to take out the VP?" he inquired to Met and Pru, but before they could reply, two rounds in quick succession struck just above Blue Jay's head. Everyone immediately hit the deck and scanned the area behind their location. Not seeing any activity and with no additional incoming rounds, Blue Jay ordered a hasty departure. After positioning the sniper rifles with the two dead men, the unit left the area.

After they had moved a safe distance away, Blue Jay brought the unit to a halt and moved them into a very heavily wooded area. "Here's the deal," Blue Jay informed the others. "The rendezvous point depends on how Bean's action goes, so you people should hold up in the general area of the other unit in case they need your support."

"What do you mean, you people?" Tic inquired.

"I'm going to look for that shooter," Blue Jay said. "Whoever it was saw our faces and may be able to ID us if captured."

"I think we're all going to look for the shooter," Tic informed him.

"No," Blue Jay ordered, as he passed the radio to the other three men. "The other unit may need your support if they have to make a hasty retreat, so move back in their direction and hold up. I won't look long and will stay up on the com. Now make a little noise as you leave and I'll move off in this direction."

The other three men weren't happy about it, but they followed his instructions.

CHAPTER 5

Part of Beans' revised plan was for him and Bris to scare off the Miami people before they got to the beach while Benz and Panda kept a close watch on the other group.

Hopefully, when the people on the boat realized their cover for the operation had been blown, they would use good sense and make a hasty retreat. On the other hand, if they decided to do something stupid, they would never reach the beach.

The powerful racing boat came to a halt just offshore. A rubber raft was put into the water; four men quickly got into it and started paddling toward shore.

"That's our cue, Bris," Bean whispered into the com. "You take the left flank; I'll take the right and try not to sink it."

The raft had barely gotten started on its journey to the beach when Bean ordered, "Let's do it," and brief whispers from an unseen source were heard.

The men in the raft immediately stopped paddling when five rounds on each side of the raft caused splashes as they hit the water. The startled crew just looked at each other until a second volley helped them make a smart decision and they started turning the raft back.

"The other group is looking for you, but can't seem to find your location," Benz informed Bean.

"Good," Bean acknowledged. "These people seem to be leaving and if this other group can't find us, they may get spooked and also leave."

Everything got extremely quiet as the other group searched in vain for Bean's unit and seemed to be getting a little concerned, when all of a sudden, a loud voice from the speedboat could be heard yelling at the raft to head back toward the beach. "That fuckin' tears it," Bean said in a low voice. "Let's give that asshole on the boat something to think about," he informed Bris and two brief bursts caused the bushes in front of them to shake a little.

After the 9mm rounds struck the speedboat, the bigmouth onboard wanted to depart immediately and leave the people in the raft, but he was overruled. That solved one problem, but firing that last burst gave their location away and the other group was starting to move on their positions.

"Company's coming," Benz informed them.

"Bris, keep an eye on the boat and make sure they leave. If they change their mind again, shoot the bigmouth."

"With pleasure," Bris confirmed.

"Benz, let the other group move on our position until you get an angle on them," Bean advised. "They probably think there are only one or two people canceled in the bush."

"Roger," was the reply.

As the men cautiously maneuvered toward Bean's position, Benz and Panda got that desired angle and, "Let's do it," was heard over the com. The silence was broken by the sounds of four loud whispers. Two from the front and two from the right front of the stalking men and 9mm rounds rained down onto their positions. It would have been extremely easy to kill the five men, but this was their lucky day and they were allowed to make a very hasty withdraw from the area. After pursuing the fleeing men with additional gunfire to make sure the five would not have time to stop and regroup in the immediate area, Bean gave the order for his unit to withdraw, and the four very quietly left the area.

Once he was a safe distance away from the site, Bean was on the radio. "You on?"

"I'm on," was the reply.

Bean immediately recognized Pru's voice and inquired, "Where is he?"

"I say, he went sightseeing, but will join us for tea later," Pru answered.

"Well, jolly good," Bean replied then wondered, *What the fuck is Blue Jay up to now?*

Not hearing any gunfire in the distance is a good sign that everything went well at the beach, Blue Jay reasoned, as he slowly moved toward his destination. He was taking a calculated guess that the shooter would take a certain route when withdrawing from the target area and was hoping to intersect the shooter. The terrain had turned into a less wooded area and Blue Jay put the trees to good use zigzagging through them and not setting up a pattern in his movements while doing it. This would make it more difficult for someone to get a clear shot if he was in anyone's scope.

As he approached a small group of bushes, he noticed how quiet it was, too quiet for his liking, so he came to a halt and knelt down to survey the area. After checking in a 360-degree radius, he decided to continue at a crawl toward the group of bushes. Once he was close to the bushes, he again stopped. *Have that old feeling somebody is here, but unless they make a move, I'm probably not going to see them, so on to plan B,* he reasoned to himself, as he slowly went into his pack and removed an old World War II hand grenade Jar Head and Doggie had given him many years ago. Holding the grenade with the lever or spoon as everyone in the military called it, facing back toward the web of his palm, he got a tight grip on the grenade as he pulled on a ring that would remove a cotter pin that held the spoon in place. On this older type grenade, once the pin was removed and the spoon was released, a small power fuse would burn down before setting off the primary charge causing an explosion that sends metal fragments in all directions with lethal results. Once the pin was removed, Blue Jay crept closer so he could observe the entire bush area. After again checking the area, he straightened out his right arm down the right side of his body, then in one motion, moved it quickly into the air toward the bushes and released the grenade. As it started a high arc toward the bushes, the telltale pinging sound of a spoon flying loose from a grenade rang out followed by white smoke from the burning fuse that would last for three to five seconds before the main charge went off. Blue Jay kept close watch on the bushes and noticed a slight movement as the last few seconds of the fuse burnt down, but this time, there was no tremendous explosion. It was a dud or a grenade with its primary charge removed.

That slight movement was the only thing Blue Jay needed as he called out, "I'ma look at the bushes. I'ma see you." When no reply came back, he clicked the selector on his MP5 to semiautomatic, aimed, and placed two rounds in a tree near the group of bushes.

"Okay, dickhead, you got me," a voice finally rang out.

"Oh, is that you, brother?" Blue Jay inquired, already knowing that was probably the case.

"Very funny," the voice again responded, as a man stood up not far from the tree.

The two men approached each other, shook hands, embraced, and Blue Jay said, "Long time no see."

"It has been a while," his brother agreed.

"How come you took out the VP?" Blue Jay inquired.

"That's what the client wanted, nothing political, but very personal," his brother answered then said, "Was surprised when you didn't take out Raul."

"Same reason, it's what the client wanted," Blue Jay replied, as the brothers eyeballed each other and smiled.

"How did you know it was me?" his brother inquired.

"Two reasons," Blue Jay replied. "A sniper with a semiautomatic weapon. See you're still using that Heckler and Koch PSG-1. But the main reason was those two rounds you put above my head."

"I was wondering if that would ring any bells," his brother mused.

"Oh, it rang some bells all right," Blue Jay confirmed. "Two kids in the woods stalking each other with BB guns. You hitting me in the head with BB's until you perfected that two shots above the head bullshit. I still have the dents in my head."

"So you did remember," his brother said with a smile.

"Yeah, I remembered," Blue Jay conceded then added, "We better get out of here. Do you need a ride?"

"No, my route will be through the mountains," his brother told him, as he bent down, picked up the grenade, then went over and picked up the spoon. "Here is your toy," he said, as he handed them to his brother.

"Made you move, didn't it?" Blue Jay replied then added, "You keep it," as he handed the pull ring with attached cotter pin to him.

"Thanks, I will," his brother said with a smile.

"Well, I better go check on the troops," Blue Jay said, once again extending his hand. "Let's touch base soon."

"Sounds good," his brother replied. "Take care."

The two departed with a good feeling. There was never any animosity between them; they just hadn't been in touch for too many years.

———————

As his brother resumed his trek toward the mountains, Blue Jay started to hustle back to the Team or at least get into com unit range. The area was starting to fill up with troops, but Blue Jay's skill set allowed him to maneuver around them without detection.

The Team had regrouped at the rendezvous point and Bean was getting a quick update from Tic about what had happened.

When Tic had finished, Bean was on the com. "You on?"

A very weak and broken up, "Yeah, I'm on," was heard probably due to him being at the maximum range for the com unit.

After waiting a few minutes, Bean again asked, "You on?"

A little stronger, "I'm on," was heard.

"Shall we wait or meet you at the Jockey Club for tea?" Bean then asked.

"Will meet you at the club for tea," was the reply.

As Blue Jay started to move toward the plane, he thought, *The Jockey Club for tea. Pru must have instigated that line somehow. It sure didn't come out of Bean's repartee.*

After talking with Blue Jay, the Team was also on their way to tea.

Cuban military had moved into the area of the villa, had probably discovered the bodies from Big Face land, and tagged them as the shooters. That would not hold up later when all of the rounds are collected and analyzed. When they discover the two that flew past Raul's head and the two in the VP were not fired from the same gun and were not even the same caliber as the two Russian sniper rifles, they would have a mystery on their hands.

If this area were closer to Havana, the area would have been saturated with troops by now. This was a good thing for the Team. It would give them much needed time to leave the island before everything was shut down tight.

As the Team neared the location of the cove, they heard voices speaking in Spanish.

"Cuban troops," Tic whispered into the com unit and everyone slowly took cover in the brush.

Still fully camouflaged, the Team members blended right into their surroundings as a Cuban patrol, having been alerted about the assassination of the VP, was moving quickly through their assigned areas looking for any signs of the person or persons responsible.

An eager young private burst into a very small clearing, but discovered nothing except a few clumps of grass and quickly continued across the clearing. Halfway across the clearing, he tripped over something that was more substantial than grass, but before he could fully recover and investigate, Panda straightened out his left arm, swung it at ground level catching the back of both heels of the man standing next to him, sending him into the air, and crashing to the ground. After a quick jab to the jaw, the private was unconscious. The Team held positions and another member of the patrol entered the clearing, saw the private on the ground, assumed he had fallen or passed out, and quickly went to his side to assist him, but the clump of grass had other ideas and now there were two unconscious men in the clearing. Having already been extremely lucky in this situation, the Team quickly moved on, but was detected just outside the clearing and that was when the shit hit the fan.

Immediately realizing these people in camouflage kill, suits didn't belong in Cuba and were probably involved in the assassination. The senior man ordered the patrol to open fire.

That was not a good decision for him and the patrol, but it did alert other patrols in the area and they reported the activity back to the villa.

The Team was again moving toward the cove and Bean was on the com. "We may have company and it will get hot, so fire it up."

"Roger," was the one-word reply.

As Jockey ran to the cockpit of the plane and started to fire up the engines, he grumbled aloud, "We had a nice peaceful place here and were enjoying ourselves, but noooo, they have to bring trouble!" he exclaimed, as the first engine started.

Check, who had set up a lookout position on the top of the cliff at the mouth of the cove, should have heard all of the communications from Bean, but unknown to him, the com unit was damaged when he climbed up onto the cliff.

More and more troops were flowing into the area as the Team bobbed and weaved their way to the plane. When they were very close to the cove, Bean was on the com assigning duties to the Team members to assure a hasty departure, when they were brought under fire. With the cracking of gunfire and incoming rounds hitting the area, everyone hit the deck and rolled or dove for the little cover that was available. *This is not good,* Bean thought to himself from behind a large tree. *We can't stay here, but moving isn't going to be easy.* Bean looked around to see the positions of the Team members then said into the com, "Tic, you and the Team crawl out to the left, then try to flank these guys while I try to keep them occupied." Tic acknowledged and the Team moved out.

Bean put a fresh mag into his MP5 then started the show first firing from one side of the tree then the other, trying not to set up any type of pattern. As Bean's second mag went dry, Tic was on the com. "We're in place," he informed him.

"Let me load a fresh mag first," Bean replied.

The man leading the ambush was no dummy. He had placed a man on both of his flanks to watch for such a move. When the man on his right flank reported movement, he alerted the men he had in position for a counterattack if they were overrun.

With the fresh mag in place, Bean was on the com. "Ready," then after a pause said, "Let's do it." He and the Team came up firing and moved quickly toward the enemy positions.

With all of those incoming rounds, the people sitting in ambush didn't put up much of a fight and fled rather quickly.

"That's strange," Bean said into the com after they had overrun the position. "Watch out for a counterattack," just came out of his mouth when it happened.

The leader of the ambush was intent on taking back the position and killing as many of his enemies as possible.

The Team went into kneeling positions after overrunning the position, but their enemy was now trying to employ the same tactic and overrun them.

The Team immediately got into the prone position and returned fire as the attacking force moved toward them. Incoming fire was intense, but then suddenly, it eased up a little.

Taking a quick look, Bean noticed men on the left side of the attacking force were dropping and immediately ordered the Team to increase their automatic weapons fire.

With the unexpected incoming fire from his left flank and the sudden surge fire from the front, the leader ordered a retreat.

As the Team watched the Cubans move back, "Can't leave you people alone for five minutes without you getting into some kind of trouble," Blue Jay's voice scolded over the com. "Come up this way, it's clear."

When the Team was again on the move, Bean asked, "How did you get up there?"

"Heard you on the com, the gunfire and changed course to this area when I ran across these turds. It looked like they were going to counterattack after the Team overran their position, so I waited," Blue Jay answered with a smile.

"What about the shooter?" Bean inquired.

"Ran out of time during the search," Blue Jay replied.

———————

A company of regulars was a very short distance away when they heard the gunfire, reported it on the radio, and were ordered to the area.

The first thing Blue Jay asked when he arrived at the plane was, "Where's Check?"

"Isn't he out there?" a concerned Air Jockey asked, as he quickly moved to the plane's doorway. "He set up on the cliff at the mouth of the cove, but I figured he came down after hearing all of the com traffic."

Blue Jay quickly moved past the plane so he could get a better look at the cliff as he inquired, "Check, you on?" When there was no reply, he assumed something was wrong with communications and started waving for him to come down. Check was already preparing to move down. After he didn't hear anything on the com when the Team showed up at the plane, he figured his com was out.

Blue Jay was still waving when incoming rounds started kicking up sand on the beach. As the Team quickly returned fire, Blue Jay ordered, "Everyone on the plane. Check will have to jump for it."

Each man maintained their fire as they backed toward the plane. Being the furthest away when it started, Blue Jay was the last to board and cut the remaining rope that secured the plane to the beach.

Jockey was in the pilot's seat with his hand on the throttles when the last man boarded. He slammed them forward. The plane moved out from under its camouflage umbrella and headed for the cove's entrance.

Check figured out the game plan and was going to jump. As the plane navigated through the cove's entrance, Jockey pulled back on the throttles so the plane would slow to a stop to pick up Check.

As he was preparing to jump, something caught his eye. A man with a rocket launcher was running down the beach to get a better position for a shot at the plane. Check immediately dropped down into the prone position and fired as the man was taking aim. When the 9mm rounds struck him, he accidentally fired the rocket and it barely missed the plane.

After the rocket exploded on the face of the cliff next to them, the Team members were a little more anxious to get Check off the top of the cliff, but he waved them on yelling, "Get the plane out of the line of fire first!"

"Good idea," Blue Jay agreed and ordered Jockey to navigate the plane out of the entrance to the left and hold position.

As the plane's engines revved up and the plane started moving, Check gave a little wave as if he were saying goodbye to the Team.

"He's planning on setting up a rear guard and sacrificing himself so we can escape!" Met yelled out to everyone.

"What!" Blue Jay barked, as he scrambled out of the co-pilot's seat in the cockpit.

"Not today," Benz advised, as he put an inflatable life vest over his head and Panda finished tying a knot in the rope that ran across Benz's chest and under each arm. Without delay, Benz moved to the door and jumped into the water. Panda took up a position in the doorway feeding out rope as Benz swam back to the center of the entrance as the plane moved away. Check was busy firing at the troops on the beach and was in the middle of changing a mag when he heard, "Get down here!" He wasn't sure what he heard, but looked down into the cove's entrance and saw Benz treading water with rounds from the beach making little smashes around his head.

Everyone in the plane saw the rounds splashing around Benz's head, but couldn't see the shooters to give fire support.

Bean surveyed the situation and then slowly climbed out the door.

"Now where are you going?" Panda inquired.

"See if I can get a better view," Bean answered, and started climbing to the roof of the plane.

Once on the roof, Bean tried to see the men firing at Benz. The seaplane was bobbing in the water and every time it bobbed up, Bean would catch a quick view of the men on the beach and fired a burst from his MP5. It didn't stop the firing from the beach, but it slowed it down a little.

"Now would be a good time!" Benz instructed. "And try not to land on me."

Check smiled, shook his head, took aim, and sprayed the beach until the last round went out the barrel then jumped into the water.

When he came to the surface, Benz was there and after inflating the vest, wrapped his arms and legs around Check.

Seeing that was done, Panda first yelled, "Hang on up there," then gave the word to the pilot and Jockey slowly eased the throttles forward until all of the slack was out of the rope, then added more power and the two men went skidding across the water.

Bean didn't really have much to hang onto, so he just laid face down, straddled the plane with arms and legs on both sides of the plane, and when the plane got up to speed, yelled, "Rock and Roll!"

Once they were at a safe distance, the plane came to a halt and the Team pulled on the rope until the two men were next to the plane. They got the two men aboard and then helped Bean to get down off the roof and back into the plane.

Once the men were onboard, Jockey pushed the throttles full forward and when the plane reached takeoff speed, eased it into the air.

"You both did a very brave thing," Blue Jay commended and the Team agreed, but both men just shrugged off the praise. Benz yelled out so Air Jockey could hear. "We could use some extra points in the Bull Shit Derby's Annual JCCF Award competition."

There was a slight pause then Jockey replied, "I'll see what I can do. It's all very hush-hush you know."

"You and your hush-hush," Check added. "Next, you'll be telling us about those fucking carrier pigeons that bring the secret votes to you."

Benz got a kick out of that statement and pushed Check on the shoulder, as he and everyone burst into laughter.

"This Annual JCCF Award has been going on for five years," Panda said. "Has anyone ever actually received the award?"

"It's virtual," Jockey immediately replied.

"You should have told us that," Panda suggested, as he shook his head and smiled.

"Okay, it's the Virtual Annual JCCF Award," Jockey agreed.

When the laughter subsided, Check said, "Thanks, Benz, I owe you one."

"Don't worry about it," Benz assured him. "Panda and I were already making preparations in case you got hit before or after you went into the water. When the rocket exploded and you waved goodbye, we just improvised."

"Yeah, he yelled, 'let's do it,' and jumped out the door," Panda confirmed with a chuckle.

"Thank you, too, Panda," Check then offered and Panda acknowledged.

"So I just jumped out the door," Benz said, as he tossed the wet life vest at Panda and both men had a hardy laugh.

The ball was now back in Air Jockey's court. He got them in, now he had to get them out.

Once again staying under 300 feet, the seaplane raced away from the Cuban coast. Blue Jay was in the co-pilot's seat constantly checking the plane's navigational instruments and their coordinates using one of JC's super duper GPS devices.

After a short period of time had passed, Blue Jay said, "Let's hang out for a while," and Jockey took the plane into a slow right turn.

It was very quiet as the plane made three more right turns then a voice over the radio broke the silence. "I know this is only your third lesson, but if you don't start shaping up, it will be the last one I'll be giving you. Do you understand?"

"Yeah," was the nervous sounding reply.

"I see Mac's part hasn't gotten any bigger," Panda observed. "He better get a talent agent and renegotiate his contract."

Everyone chuckled as Jockey and Blue Jay searched the sky above for the other seaplane. "I think that's them at our nine o'clock," Blue Jay advised.

Jockey eased the plane to the left for a better look and soon confirmed it was them.

"Click the mike," he said and Blue Jay pressed and released the send button twice.

When there was no reply, Jockey said, "They're looking. Maybe a little motion will help them locate us." He dipped the right then the left wing. A short time later, two clicks were heard over the radio.

"Well, we are already in position, so it's up to JC to start the show," Air Jockey advised.

"And now Crazy and The Man from Pussy Airways will perform their death defying aerobatics," Panda announced. "How do I get talked into these things?" He then made a fake plead to the Team.

"Fuck you, peckerhead!" Jockey quickly responded from the pilot's seat, as he kept a sharp eye on the other seaplane.

"Okay, I'm giving you the control of the plane," JC announced over the radio, as he calculated his next move. "That's good," he continued with the make-believe dialogue.

JC had positioned his aircraft so it approached the other craft high and to their left. "Now let's make a slow turn to your left," JC suggested then he made an abrupt turn and pointed the nose of the plane downward as it turned. "Keep the nose up," he ordered.

This maneuver was nothing out of the ordinary for new students who usually failed to keep the nose up when learning how to turn an aircraft. "I said keep the nose up." JC gave the more urgent order, as he kept close watch on his altimeter and at the same time, straining for a look at the other plane.

Keeping close watch on the other plane's left turn, Jockey estimated where he should be and moved the throttles of his plane forward.

When he was below 300 feet, JC leveled off and yelled into the radio, "Give me the controls!" and after catching sight of the other plane, banked his plane a little to the right, then pulled back the throttles to allow Jockey to get into position. In order to allow Jockey time to get into position and to make sure no one thought they had crashed, JC was again scolding the student while Mac was straining to catch sight of the other plane.

Mac finally signaled they were in position and JC gave the planned signal that he was about to climb to a respectable altitude. "I'll never take you out flying again; we're going back."

With that said, JC put his craft into a gradual climb as Jockey did the same. When they reappeared as a blip on the radarscope, they looked like one plane heading back toward the Bahamas.

"Is it over yet?" Panda inquired with his hands covering his eyes.

"Yes, it's over," the Team played along.

"Did we crash?" was his next question.

"No!"

"Good," Panda replied, as he removed his hands from over his eyes.

"Don't you think you're flying a bit too close?" Blue Jay inquired.

"Noooo, flying this close is cake," Jockey assured Blue Jay who just shook his head.

"You all lied, it's not over," Panda complained, as he again covered his eyes.

"I wouldn't distract the man from Pussy Airways if I were you," Blue Jay suggested. "If we get any closer, we're going to look like one of those cartoons where a plane's propeller saws through the ass end of the plane in front of it."

Panda was batting a thousand. He always managed to get things stirred up especially to and from a Project. This time, it looked like more laughter than usual was in store for the Team.

CHAPTER 6

The Team members took the usual furlough time after a Project and they were again in residence at the Barn.

The Board had already been in session at JJ's suite of offices in Manhattan and completed a review of the last Project. There was a great amount of concern about the shooter that took out the vice president, but it still remained a mystery. With no group claiming responsibility, plus with Raul and the news media somehow getting information about the vice president's financial accounts and his arrangements with a foreign power, the matter would just fade away with time.

The Board had also considered three proposed Projects. They held meetings until they selected one that JJ and Mac would present to the Team for their approval. The Board members had struggled a great deal before selecting this Project and finally only agreed because of its extreme importance. They all knew the Team had the last word and could vote the Project down.

JJ and Mac had scheduled a meeting to present the next Project and one day later, the Team members were filing into the Team meeting room at the Barn.

When everyone was seated, JJ brought the meeting to order. "Morning, gentlemen. I hope you all had an enjoyable furlough?" He got a group yes in reply.

"This next undertaking may require a different approach compared to our previous Projects," he started. "As we all know, our original planning for operations was as follows. Team, units, pairs or just one man, but to date, most of the Projects were at the Team level and have been very successful.

"In the beginning, we used to present a high level plan from the Board, but quickly realized it would get changed and customized. The final plan sometimes didn't even resemble the original or as Mac put it, 'Why submit a plan, they'll just shit can the plan and start over anyway.'"

JJ paused as the Team chuckled and he prepared to give his part of the presentation.

As in the past, he would give a high overview and Mac would follow up with a more detailed presentation.

"I'll start off by giving you a little background information," JJ started again. "As you all know, Alexander Litvinenko was assassinated in London several months ago and Polonium 210 was used as the weapon. I know you'll all agree that using a radioactive substance was a highly unusual way to eliminate a person unless somebody was really pissed off and wanted revenge or was trying to send a message or was trying to implicate a third party in the death.

"The Kremlin seemed to be a good candidate. In the past, they have been known to do some nasty things to people. When CIA's traitor Aims turned over names to the KGB of people that were working for the west, they did some of those types of things like putting a general into an industrial furnace feet first while he was still alive and that was after he had been retired for years.

"Another candidate could be a Russian businessman looking for revenge and at the same time, pointing a finger back at the Kremlin. Apparently, Litvinenko created a dossier on that man for an English firm that cost the businessman millions when the deal fell through. That same businessman is also under indictment in Russia, living in England where there is no extradition treaty, and in the past, tried to bring down the Puton government.

"Whoever was responsible, it's up to Scotland Yard to figure out. We are not in the crime fighting business, but I wanted to make you aware of the types that could be involved with the Polonium 210. If there are no questions, I'll turn it over to Mac." After a few seconds, he motioned to Mac.

"Morning, people. First of all, I'd like to inform some of you I now have a talent agent to negotiate for better parts in any upcoming Projects," Mac said, as he looked straight at Panda who at the same time was looking around at the others trying to figure out who Mac could be talking about.

"Keep looking, Panda, you'll figure it out," Mac said with a smile.

"On a more serious note, I would like to again commend all of you for a job well done and especially to Benz and Check for their heroic actions and dedication to other Team members. Only wish I had medals to award you both," General Mac added in a sincere voice.

"Hear, hear," Pru announced, as he and the other Team members stood and applauded the two men.

Check and Benz were touched by the words and the Team's reaction, as they both smiled and looked at each person in the room.

When things quieted down, Mac resumed his presentation. "As JJ said, we are not in the crime fighting business, but sometimes crime and terrorist paths do cross. We have reason to believe that may have occurred in the Litvinenko matter. We have it from a good source that person or persons in an old Soviet block country may have sold Polonium 210 to someone involved in the Litvinenko assassination. Apparently, the sellers are too careless or do not know how to handle it properly and unknowingly, the buyers have been leaving a trail of low radiation. I'm sure you all remember seeing in the media during the investigation that radiation was detected in a London hotel, restaurant, apartment, and on airliners. We're guessing that most of those discoveries all have to do with the killing, but in the cases of the airliners, there were just too many aircraft with too many regular destinations to have all been caused by the London assassins, and that brings us to the Project," Mac said, as he took a sip of water.

"This time, if the Team votes to accept it, the Project would involve travel to several countries in Europe to follow up on leads, gather intelligence, and report it back. The incoming intelligence would be analyzed to first verify then try to piece it together with other incoming information. If we discover the sales of Polonium 210 are being made to the terrorists, we would take action.

"Our source, regardless of our decision about the Project, will continue to pursue the matter in an old Soviet block country, but they lack the manpower to perform Intel gathering in other countries."

Mac and the Board knew the very reliable source was Dunn, but didn't know the field sources were Rene and Boris. Gil still followed the rule of "on a need to know basis" from his days at the CIA and never told the Board about any of his sources.

Rene fell into that category and even though he had worked behind the scenes on several Projects in the past, Dunn never shared his identity with the Board. The most they ever knew was that Gil got on the phone and things happened.

Gil and Rene even used the "on a need to know basis" with each other and neither ever had a problem with it. The fact that Boris was now working on a third Project with Rene and that Gil didn't know about him until recently showed how the rule worked and the amount of trust the men shared in each other.

Mac was winding down his presentation. "As in the past, you will now hold meetings to consider the Project before giving the Team's decision and if your answer is yes, we'll have another meeting giving more detailed information.

"I personally feel you should take your time before deciding on this one. For one thing, it will require a different mode of operation for the Team. That said, are there any questions?" Mac inquired.

"Qualify, we'll take action?" JC asked.

"Once we have gotten all of the Intel we can, decisions will have to be made at that time," Mac replied. "If we feel the ongoing activity is located in a country that will take action, we'll make sure they are made aware of it. If not, we'll take another course of action."

After satisfying a few more questions, Mac asked, "Anyone else?" When no one responded, he ended the briefing.

When JJ and Mac left the room, the Team started deliberation about the Project. As the two men walked back to the house, JJ inquired, "You have a bad feeling about this one?"

"Why do you ask?" Mac replied.

"Out of all of the briefings we have given the Team, that was the first time I ever heard you express a personal feeling in the area of caution."

"Like I said, it's a change in their MO," Mac replied. "For over five years, we have functioned mostly as a Team."

"Well, maybe they will decide to pass if they don't feel comfortable with it," JJ reasoned.

"Maybe," Mac agreed, "but not likely."

———————

The Team did take more time than usual to make their decision, then all agreed to take on the Project and were in the Team meeting room for the detailed briefing.

Mac was standing next to a large map of Europe that was positioned at the front of the room when he started the briefing. "Morning, men," Mac started and got a group reply. "As I said in the past, if we give you a plan, you'll just shit can it anyway, so I'll just give you the facts as we know them.

"To start with, let me fill in some of the holes. We said at the first briefing, the sale of Polonium 210 was occurring in an old Soviet block country and that country is the Republic of Georgia. We also talked about a source that supplied that information. I can't really get into too much detail about that, but can say someone on the Board has close ties with that source and it is very sensitive. To tell the truth right now, you know about as much as I do."

The Team chuckled and understood the need for security. Not too many people should have in-depth knowledge about the organization. That could be a dangerous thing if the wrong people were on the Board and Team. The Board could use the

Team for reasons other than good while convincing the Team it was okay. In this case, there was no need for worry. The Board was honorable and the Team didn't have to worry. However, if that ever changed, the Board itself would become a Project for the Team.

"About all I can do is restate what we said in the first briefing." Mac continued. "The source will continue their Intel work in Georgia and they do need help following the trail to other countries. At present, we have several countries that may or may not be part of the trail. Britain could be part of the trail or it may just look that way because of the Polonium 210 being used in the assassination, but at present, there are too many law enforcement and intelligence types on the scene for us to poke our noses in there."

"Oh, hard cheese," Pru commented, "and I was looking forward to looking in on old Granny."

"Well, tell Granny to keep the kettle on," Mac advised, "because things may turn in that direction."

"Good show," Pru approved of Mac's Brit humor, as the Team chuckled.

"Through our people in the Republic of Georgia, plus other sources, we have so far identified three countries in the trail: France, Germany, and Spain. If the terrorists are purchasing Polonium 210, their target will probably be a western country. The question is will it be a European country or the US… It goes without saying when picking up the trail in these countries we have to verify the lead is legitimate then try to determine if that country is a target itself or just a distributed collection point. I realize this is a lot to ask, but the stakes are very high.

"Polonium 210 used as a dirty weapon set off by other explosives in a large urban area or a sudden outbreak of radiation poisoning being reported in the media could cause public panic.

Politicians may even feel forced to do something like nuke the most likely candidate that supported the terrorist group responsible. Polonium 210 can also be used as part of a trigger to set off a nuclear bomb. The bottom line is, Polonium 210 is being sold, and we have to find out whom the buyers are.

"Are there any questions or concerns?" Mac asked.

"Have two questions," JC spoke up. "What action would be taken if the trail leads to the government of a country?"

"I'd say we cut off the source and inform the world community about the sales to that country," Mac answered, as he looked at JJ who agreed with the statement.

"If the Team accepts the Project, could Swabbie, Jar Head, and Doggie join us again in the planning sessions?" JC asked his second question. "It worked out really well the last time."

"I'll ask them," Mac replied.

"Oh, they'll agree," Blue Jay spoke up. "Those hambones wouldn't be able to resist the opportunity of putting in their two cents."

"Plus, they would have the added bonus of pestering the shit out of the two of us," Bean added.

Mac, JJ, and the Team all laughed at the remarks knowing that last statement was especially true.

———————

The planning sessions got off to a flying start. The Team, along with their three additions, was putting together a plan in record time. The financial and other requirements were very demanding, but as in the past, the Board had no complaints when JJ or Mac presented requirements at their meetings.

The atmosphere in the Team room did start to get bogged down in planning once until Jar Head announced that he was informed that certain people on the Team had referred him and his two associates as hambones and that they would be pestering the shit out of people. That started an exchange that picked up the pace in the planning and it never slowed down again.

With planning and preparations completed, JC would brief everyone to make sure nothing had been overlooked. "Morning, people," JC started. "As you know, we're going to make a pass over this plan to make sure we didn't miss anything. JJ and Mac, please feel free to question anything. The rest of us have been deeply involved in the planning and sometimes in a situation like that, the obvious can be overlooked.

"Phase one will be to set up a forward home base in Luxembourg. An advance party will depart a day prior to the main group to check out the airport, new home base itself, etcetera. The following day, Jockey will transport the remainder to Luxembourg International Airport on the new Global Express business jet. Jockey convinced the powers that be that this was the way to go. More range - over seven thousand miles, more seats - ten to fourteen, more speed - over five hundred miles per hour, and it can land on primary as well as poorer quality airstrips. Well done, just what the doctor ordered," JC said as he motioned toward Jockey then JJ.

"We will be using a renovated eighteenth century farm house as home base. It is a remote location, but not that far from the airport. We will settle in, establish communications with the Barn, and check for any updated information. Code names Mr. Blue and Mr. Black will be handling Intel, be in communication with the folks at the Barn, and they will relay the information to us.

"Phase two. We plan to send three two-man units into the countries in question. Met and Pru to Germany, Tic and Check to Spain, Bris and Jockey to France. Blue Jay, Bean, Benz, and Panda will be held in reserve and act as other units or as an action force for the other three units.

"Each unit has been training with the man that will be receiving their reports from the field. Swabbie-Germany, Jar Head-France, and Doggie-Spain.

"Since these three men will be with us, we felt it better if their wives moved into the house at the Barn with Top, LadyA and Lady1.

"When the reports are received from the units, they will be reviewed and analyzed by everyone at the forward home base. If we see a pattern or a trail leading somewhere else, we can relocate the unit or employ one or both of the units we kept in reserve.

"Phase three. If we feel there is nothing to corroborate the Intel about the Polonium 210 trail, we'll recall that unit to home base. If terrorist activity is discovered, but no Polonium 210 trail, they will also be recalled. The activity will be documented and the Board can decide what they want to do about it at a later date. We have to keep our eye on the ball with no distractions and the ball is the Polonium 210 trail.

"Phase four will depend on how things play themselves out. We have planned for several different courses of action for each situation.

"I am assuming the source currently in the Republic of Georgia will handle their part whatever the decision may be." JC gestured toward JJ.

"Unless there is an unforeseen problem, we can say they will not require assistance," JJ assured him.

JC continued the briefing taking each phase into greater detail. After another hour had passed, JC decided it was time to let the information sink in a little. "Think it's time to take a break," he announced. "Are there any questions?"

After a silent pause, Mac spoke up. "I wasn't aware that Jockey spoke French."

"Wee wee," Jockey yelled and waved his hand in the air.

"Yes, yes," Mac translated the two French words. "Very good."

"It's what I have to do," Jockey advised. "Teacher, teacher, I have to go wee-wee."

The Team burst into laughter, as Mac looked at Jockey and admitted, "I should have known."

"Can't wait to see how this humor goes over in France, especially if we get to Paris. Bet he'll be a big hit with the Parisians," Bris guessed.

"Really," Jockey inquired.

"No, they don't even like other French people," Bris quickly answered.

"Oh well," Mac observed, "French – American relations weren't that great to start with, but they'll probably really go into the shitter now."

"Maybe we should dress him up like Hop-Sing," Benz suggested, "then the French would get mad at China."

"Oh, that's funny," Jockey commented, "and the secret committee had such high hopes for you getting points toward the Annual JCCF Award."

"The Virtual Annual JCCF Award," Panda corrected.

"And if I want any shit out of you, I'll squeeze your head," Jockey explained to Panda.

JC knew control was lost and the best thing to do was to call out, "Coffee break!"

The message went almost unnoticed as the Team went into verbal warfare, but when someone noticed JC walking out, they assumed he was going for coffee and alerted the others who continued verbal skirmishes to and from the coffee pot.

CHAPTER 7

It was 8:47 P.M. when Jockey taxied the Express Business Jet to a stop in front of a private hangar at Luxembourg International Airport. After the door of the jet was swung open, two men approached the aircraft pushing a portable staircase, placed it in front of the door, and locked it into place. "Good service at this airport," JJ remarked then started down the stairs. When he got to the bottom, one of the men put his hand to the bill of his cap as he relieved JJ of his briefcase and said, "Transportation is waiting, sir." Then pointed to the two vans parked by the hangar.

JJ thanked the man and proceeded toward the first van followed by the other passengers. When Jockey got to the bottom of the stairs, he said, "Oh, boy!" and pointed to the briefcase he just placed on the ground. The other man quickly proceeded to assist Jockey, put his hand to the bill of his cap, picked up the briefcase, and said, "Yes, sir, right this way," pointing toward the vans. As he turned, the briefcase banged against Jockey's leg.

"I'm sorry, sir," Panda said with fake sincerity. "Are you all right?"

"Fine, fine," Jockey replied, "just walk in front of me. Must be hard to find good help over here, too," he complained.

Nothing out of the ordinary to remove from the plane prior to departing the airport. JC, Benz, and Panda had brought the out of the ordinary items with them on the smaller Lear Jet the day before and had already transported them to home base.

After the two vans were loaded, they left the airport and were en route to the converted farmhouse when JJ inquired, "Any problems with the residence?"

"No," Panda answered, as he navigated the van to its destination. "As an SOP, we swept the house for any type of devices and it was clean. We noticed very little traffic in the area and that will aid us in keeping the site secure. As you already know, JC established communications with the Barn and three hours ago got an update on the Project. He plans to brief everyone after we arrive."

"And the vehicles?" JJ then asked.

"That also went well. We transported all of the vehicles to home base prior to taking up residence. Did that first to make sure someone would always be at home base after we swept and secured it."

"Good," JJ acknowledged. He knew his inquiries were unnecessary, but asked out of a force of habit from his corporate days. The conversation made JJ think about the Team and how they functioned. One minute joking around and the next very professional.

JJ was deep in thought with a smile on his face when he heard Panda say, "We turn off the main road right up here."

As JJ looked out the front window, the van was turning onto a secondary road that immediately started to climb and after negotiating a series of curves, they were turning onto the lane that led to home base.

When the vans came to a halt, JC was outside to greet everyone. "Good flight I hope," JC wished, as he and JJ walked toward the house.

"Yes, it was," JJ confirmed. "The new plane made it an exceptionally good flight."

"And how was your flight in that cramped up little Lear jet?" Jockey asked Panda.

"Well, after Wildman performed a loop-de-loop and buzzed two tuna boats, it wasn't bad," Panda replied. "I could say more, but I don't want to contribute to the ongoing Wildman humor about the way JC pilots an aircraft."

"Yeah, I know," Jockey said with a chuckle, responding to the creator of the Wildman humor.

With everyone in the house, JC guided them to the kitchen where he had refreshments waiting. After everyone had gotten coffee or a beverage of choice and were sitting or standing in the kitchen, JC got everyone's attention. "We received an update," he said in a loud voice and the group immediately got quiet. "Our sources now have reason to believe that Italy should be added to the countries in question. I realize this is an unexpected turn of events. Our contingency planning covered other countries with a high probability of being in the trail. Unfortunately, Italy wasn't one of them." JC paused then resumed. "We have additional units available, but I guess the first logical question is does anyone speak Italian?"

At first, the group remained quiet, but then a voice asked, "Which dialect?" and everyone turned to look at Jar Head who was standing with his hand in the air.

"Do you speak the language?" JC inquired.

"Yes, and so does Doggie," Jar Head replied.

Realizing no one else had the skills, JC quickly advised, "Maybe we should take this offline," not wanting to embarrass the retired agents if the decision was not favorable.

"JJ, Mac, Swabbie, Bean, and Blue Jay, will you all join us," JC asked, as he moved toward the doorway on his way to the front room of the house.

"As soon as he said Italy, I was afraid this was going to happen," Blue Jay whispered to Bean, as the two lagged behind the others.

"I know," Bean said in agreement. "How are we going to play this?"

"By ear I guess."

When everyone was seated, JC started. "First, let me make sure I am correct in assuming you are volunteering?"

"Yes, I guess you could say that," Jar Head replied and Doggie agreed.

"I don't want to be disrespectful, but you two have been retired for some time, haven't you?"

"Yes," Doggie answered, "but we were already old when we took retirement."

"No, that's not what I meant," JC smiled, as the Duo started doing what they do best, getting their way.

He asked a few more questions then Mac and JJ continued with their concerns as JC gave the matter some thought. *They have been retired for a while, but when we executed that rescue operation on Corsica a while back, they did manage to blow the shit out of the bad guys' helicopter when he was trying to escape.*

Swabbie, Bean, and Blue Jay had seen them in action many times in past years at the Agency, but this time, all were torn between wanting them to be successful and personal feelings for their safety.

When JJ and Mac had finished, JC inquired, "Does anyone else have anything they would like to add?" When no one spoke up, he added, "Think maybe the best way to resolve this would be by vote?"

When everyone agreed, JC started and voted yes followed by a yes from Mac and JJ.

Then before voting, Swabbie said, "I feel you two are getting a little long in the tooth to do something like this. Therefore, I give a conditional yes. The condition is I go with you."

Jar Head and Doggie immediately replied with an, "I don't think so."

"Well, I guess you won't be going because I can tell by the looks on their faces those two will be voting no. That means a tie and you don't go anywhere," Swabbie quickly replied.

Bean and Blue Jay, who were deep in thought, trying to decide on their yes or no vote, were caught completely off guard and before they could regroup, Jar Head and Doggie agreed with Swabbie's demand and the yes vote carried the day.

Not only did Jar Head and Doggie get their way, but also so did Swabbie.

Blue Jay looked at Bean and said, "These slick fuckers."

"We were so intent on watching those two, this other peckerhead outmaneuvered all of us," Bean replied.

The vote completed, everyone was heading back to the kitchen and were filing past Blue Jay and Bean who were still discussing the change of events.

"Don't feel bad, lads," Doggie's voice interrupted their conversation.

"Yeah, you were just up against superior minds," Swabbie advised.

"When will these children ever learn," Jar Head inquired, as all three left the room laughing.

"Does this bring back any memories from the past?" Blue Jay asked Bean.

"Yeah, in polite company they would call it an attack of sciatica, but it's really just a big pain in the ass."

When everyone was back in the kitchen, JC announced, "Jar Head, Doggie, and Swabbie will be the unit going to Italy and the units in reserve will be taking on their responsibilities at home base. That shouldn't cause any problems since we already plan and train redundancy into all phases of our Projects."

"Changes are as follows: Bean - Germany, Panda - France, Benz – Spain, and Blue Jay – Italy. Any questions?" JC asked. When no one spoke up, he suggested, "Maybe the units should meet with their new and old receivers to make sure everyone is on the same page."

Each unit with new and old receivers had huddled up, decided to go find a place they could meet, and were in the process of leaving the kitchen, but Blue Jay just took a seat at the table. "Aren't you going to meet with anyone?" Bean inquired.

"I'm meeting with the Sciatica Brothers after they are done with the other units," he replied.

"They show no respect and never have," Jar Head said with a smile, referring back to their days at the Agency.

"Can that be called age discrimination?" Doggie inquired with a chuckle.

"No, it's just stating facts," Blue Jay replied. "Individually, you are just a pain in the ass, but together you are sciatica."

With that, the three older men burst into laughter, knowing this time they had really pissed off the Duo. Oh, well, payback is a bitch, even if they are thirteen years in the coming. That made the score, Old Guys - 9, Duo - 1,000,002.

The next morning after breakfast, everyone was preparing for the departures of the units. They would not leave in a bunch, but rather spread out over the day. Since the Spain unit had the furthest to go, Tic and Check would leave first, followed by Met and Pru, then Bris and Jockey. Due to the last minute addition, the Italy unit probably wouldn't leave until late afternoon. The advance people had picked up vehicles that would be used for France and Germany; those two units had them packed up and ready to go. Using one of the vans, Benz and Panda would transport Tic and Check to the train station for their trip to Spain.

The unit going to Italy would also travel by train and was grumbling about it. "Just another reason to be pissed off at the terrorists," Jar Head complained. "Back in the day, all you needed was a weapon made of porcelain to get passed the metal detectors at airports. Now a porcelain gun wouldn't be able to get passed all those X-ray machines, so we have to ride the choo-choo train."

"Am I hearing this right?" Blue Jay inquired to Bean, as both stood in the doorway. "The superior minds are complaining about their mode of transportation."

"Not surprised," Bean said knowingly. "Back in the day, it was made all too easy for them and they got spoiled."

"Yeah, you're right," Blue Jay agreed then inquired, "Excuse me, gentlemen. Would you all like to reconsider your trip to Italy because you're not being carried to the mission on pillows?"

"Would you like to kiss our asses?" Doggie inquired.

"And they seem to be getting testy as well. My, my," Bean observed.

"Don't give us any of that shit," Jar Head exploded. "You were with us back in the day!"

"I can't seem to remember that," Blue Jay confessed. "Can you, Bean?"

"I think it was all just so easy. We've blocked it out of our memory," Bean observed.

"Yeah, well block this," Doggie informed them, as he threw an empty coffee cup at them.

After they caught the coffee cup, the Duo proceeded down the hall laughing and said, "It is like the old days."

"It is you know," Swabbie admitted. "For a second, I thought we were all back in my office at the Agency."

The other two men shook their heads in agreement and smiled as they also remembered those days.

It was time for the first unit to depart and everyone had gathered in the kitchen when JJ's voice could be heard over the others. "May I have your attention," he requested.

"First of all, I want to thank you all for how quickly and professionally you prepared for this Project. Prior to starting the Projects, we said this type of operation may be required, but for the first five years, the Projects were always at the Team level and mostly in rural or remote areas. Have to tell you, the Board and I were hesitant to even consider this one, but with the potential destruction of innocent lives hanging in the balance, we did, then as in the past, let you all make the final decision.

"I'm not going to drag this out, but it goes without saying all of our prayers and best wishes go with you all." JJ then shook hands with Tic and Check who were about to leave.

Everyone else wished the two good luck as Panda and Benz led them toward the door and the waiting van outside.

As hours passed, the remaining Team members would again gather in the kitchen as first Met and Pru, then Bris and Jockey departed.

It was late in the day by the time the unit for Italy had been updated on all of the available Intel and was prepared to leave. As everyone again gathered in the kitchen, JJ again wished the departing men good luck and thanked the trio.

"It's like riding a bike," Doggie assured him. "You never forget how."

"With maybe the exception of the sailor," Jar Head added.

"Hey! Don't give me any shit," Swabbie fired back. "Remember, I'm going only because I exercised my superior wit over you two."

"Now they're starting to nitpick," Blue Jay intervened. "Let's get this show on the road." He and Bean started making motions with their arms and hands as if they were herding chickens.

"How did we get stuck on Uncle Fudd's patrol?" Bean asked his partner.

As the kitchen door closed, Jar Head was heard complaining. "They show no respect and never have."

"Afraid it's going to be a noisy ride to the train station," JC observed, as all smiled and agreed.

JJ, Mac, JC, Benz, and Panda watched from the front window of the house as the van made its way down the long lane to the road. "I hate Projects like this," JJ confided to the others. "In the past, when we were with the Team or in the general area, it wasn't too bad, but being this far away and this time with only two-man units out there, that nagging feeling is starting to come back about me being responsible for putting so many people at risk."

"I know what you're saying about the staying back and waiting part," General Mac agreed. "You never get used to it. As for the other part, look at it this way. If we all didn't want to be in this fight, none of us would be here. You just had the idea and means to get it started and we thank you."

JJ was taken aback by his statement. Mac was not one to be that serious and only was when being very sincere.

"Thank you, Mac," JJ said, appreciating the words.

"Besides, they will be running down leads that may lead nowhere," Mac assured him.

That statement may be true, but all of the men knew it probably wasn't. With Dunn's sources now sitting on the distribution point of the Polonium 210 and other sources identifying Al-Qaeda cells as possibly having access to that Polonium 210, one or more of the leads were bound to be fruitful.

CHAPTER 8

The leads supplied to the units consisted of addresses and photographs of people that may be somehow involved with the Polonium 210. It was the job of each unit to determine the best way to monitor the situation. JC had supplied them with eavesdropping devices and other gear to assist them in their efforts.

Since their assignment was located in neighboring France, Bris and Jockey were the first to arrive at the address of their lead. The small house in Strasbourg, France was nestled amongst other small houses and after surveying the area, the unit felt confident a listening device would work out well and proceeded to get lodging nearby so they could also observe the dwelling.

———————

The German unit was the second to arrive at their lead's address in Stuttgart, but weren't as lucky as their Teammates in France.

This house was in the middle of a large field with not even a tree on the property. After checking out the area, the two men found lodging at a small inn that was within eyeshot of the house. Pru and Met talked for over an hour on the best way to proceed when Met said, "I wonder?" and disappeared into the bedroom.

Pru didn't question, he knew Met was onto something so he just poured another cup of tea and waited for his return.

Seconds later, Met reappeared with a spotter scope he had in his luggage. "Force of habit," he explained, as he held it up for his partner to see.

"Jolly good idea," Pru approved, "if we can get the correct angle."

With that scope, one could see the bullet holes in a target over 1,000 yards away and the house couldn't be more than a half mile from the inn.

Met extended the legs on a small tripod, placed it on a table, then attached the scope to it. He picked up the table and placed it in the middle of the room in front of the window where Pru was ready with a chair. After sitting in the chair, Met focused the scope and stated, "Yeah, this will work, but it's not the best."

"We'll make do," Pru assured him.

———————

After they rented a car at the train station in Madrid, Spain, Tic and Check proceeded to the address of their lead. They didn't have a house location to consider, but rather an old, but quaint, hotel on the outskirts of the city. "This is going to be interesting," Tic said, as he and Check looked the area over.

"How about if you play the part of a drunk like you did in South America that time," Check suggested. "Look, you have a bench in front of the hotel and everything."

"Very funny," Tic replied, and then added, "I guess our first step will be to check in."

The two men entered the lobby and proceeded to the front desk to check in. The people that supplied the lead also knew the number of the suite of rooms and Tic had tried to get rooms close to them when he made the reservation, but was unsuccessful.

Tic talked a mile a minute with the desk staff as Check surveyed the lobby and the people passing by.

When Tic had finished talking and laughing with the staff, a bellhop arrived to take their luggage to their suite of rooms. Check didn't speak Spanish, but knew Tic thanked them several times as they left the desk area. Once upstairs, Check thought the bellhop stopped in front of the wrong door, but a quick look from Tic notified him it was all right.

After getting a large tip, the young man left the room and Tic started to update Check via pen and paper. *This suite is next to the lead people. We had better check out the rooms before we talk. They may have listening devices in here.*

Check shook his head in agreement, as both men carefully checked the walls and everything in the room.

As they searched, Tic told him, "My parents and I stayed in this suite of rooms when I was just a kid." He relayed the story he told the desk clerk to get the rooms. "We were on our first vacation to Spain; I'll never forget it."

"And they say Bris is the artist," Check said to Tic in a low voice after the rooms were checked.

"It's a gift," Tic admitted. "I got the suite, now you can install the pinhole mike while I take a siesta."

"Yes, I'm sure all of that bull tired you out," Check acknowledged, "and I don't mean fighting one."

Tic chuckled as he looked out the window to check out the grounds around the hotel. Hoping he could pull off getting rooms next to the lead, Tic also had diagrams of the rooms in the hotel. He and Check studied them to decide the best place to position the pinhole mike so they could listen to the conversation in the next suite. After agreeing and making reasonably sure no one was in the rooms, they installed the mike and started their surveillance.

Jar Head had stopped complaining and was enjoying the visit to the Italian Riviera, as the unit kept close watch on a seagoing yacht tied up at the Sovona port. "Big money there," Doggie observed, as he motioned toward the yacht from their suite's balcony.

"Looks like oil money to me," Swabbie observed.

"You're probably right," Jar Head agreed, "but you know it isn't connected in any way to oil money on paper. Any prince that supports terrorism also knows how to cover his tracks in all ways."

"I wonder which one's money is behind it?" Doggie pondered.

Another uneventful morning was about to end while Rene kept the site under surveillance from the bedroom window. Boris was making coffee in the little kitchenette when a knock came at the door. After alerting Rene, he went to see who was knocking. As Boris started to open the door, three men pushed their way into the room knocking him backward.

"What's going on?" Boris inquired.

"Shut up," a young punk ordered, as one of the other men went looking around the other rooms.

"Get out of here," the two men ordered Rene and he slowly obliged.

When both men were in the room, a fourth man entered through the door and closed it. "We want to ask you a few questions," the fourth man stated, obviously being the leader of the other three.

"Who do you think you are bursting in here?" Boris demanded.

"I said shut up," the young punk ordered, as he grabbed Boris by the shirt.

"Do I know you?" the leader asked Boris.

"I don't know," Boris replied, already realizing this man was a subordinate during his KGB days then quickly added, "This man is an author and he is here writing a story. I am acting as guide and translator."

"If you are writing, where is it?" the man asked Rene.

Rene understood what he said, but pretended he didn't since Boris said he was his translator.

"It's on that laptop computer," Boris quickly answered and one of the other men flipped open the PC.

As the PC was starting up, the leader inquired, "Where is the story located?"

"Microsoft Word," Boris answered.

After getting into Microsoft Word, the man reported there were no files and the leader gave a hard look at Boris who calmly went into his shirt pocket, produced a small disk, and asked, "May I?"

The man granted his request; Boris inserted the floppy disk, clicked on the correct button, then storyline, and the screen filled with text.

"Yes, I do know you," the man said, not giving anymore details.

"I am surprised you are doing something like this," the man admitted.

"The old days are gone," Boris admitted, referring to the fall of the Soviet Union and the KGB. "One does what one has to."

"True," the man admitted. "I've been reduced to babysitting a criminal activity across the street. I'm here because a hotel employee reported you two may be watching their activities for the competition."

"Really," Boris inquired to the man. "Did they tell you we are checking out this afternoon?"

"No," the leader replied.

"That's strange," Boris wondered aloud, then asked Rene in French, "Didn't you tell the front desk we would be leaving this afternoon?"

"I thought that was your job!" Rene snapped back.

"Parisian," Boris remarked, and then said, "must have had a missed communication. We are checking out this afternoon and moving on to Batumi."

"Let's go," the leader ordered the other three then extended his hand to Boris and as they shook hands, said, "Good seeing you again, Colonel."

"You, too, Major," Boris said, as both men smiled.

Boris and Rene just looked at each other without speaking when the door closed. Boris picked up the phone and informed the front desk that they would be leaving that afternoon.

While Rene started packing, Boris watched out the window to try to catch sight of the major and his three friends. After a short time, Boris moved away from the window, started packing, and motioned to Rene that they all went into a storefront across the street.

Not wanting to look like they were in too much of a rush, Rene and Boris checked out at the desk, put their luggage into their rented car, and then went into the hotel dining room for lunch. Before departing, they returned to the hotel's front desk and asked if anyone could recommend a good hotel in Batumi. They took the advice of one of the people and made a reservation using the phone at the front desk.

When they were on the road for about an hour, Boris pulled the car to the side of the road and the two men started looking for homing or listening devices in, around the car, and in their luggage.

When none was found, Boris started the conversation. "As you probably figured out, the leader of that group was a former KGB major and he may or may not be telling the truth about babysitting a criminal activity, but we can't afford to stick around to find out. I know from force of habit he will check back with his source at the hotel for any additional information about us. That's why I made our reservations from the desk at the hotel. The major will almost definitely call the other hotel to confirm that we arrived and checked in. If he is just babysitting, that will be the end of it, but if it's not, he will keep tabs on me until I leave the country."

"You better contact our friends and ask if they want us to eliminate the Polonium 210 operation or just walk away. And tell them to decide quickly because we have to leave Georgia within the next two days."

Since the units had departed from home base, everyone had settled into a routine. Except for daily reports coming in from

Stuttgart, Madrid, Strasbourg, and Savona, things at home base were pretty quiet.

Everyone communicated via coded text messages and each unit had a different time of the day assigned for routine daily reporting. If anything out of the ordinary occurred, it would be reported immediately by text or by the secure phone systems that were in place.

Everyone was in the makeshift operations center when all conversation was brought to a halt by an incoming message from the Barn in New Jersey. As JC read the message, then started to decode it, Mac remarked, "That's out of the norm, bet it's something hot."

When JC finished, he read the decoded message to the group. "Action will be taken in Georgia soon. Notify all units to be alert for unusual movement and report ASAP."

"Code that up for each unit and send it out," JC then instructed.

———————

Boris and Rene had driven to Batumi, checked into the hotel that was recommended, and after a night's sleep, were back on the road again. They knew if they checked out of the hotel, the major might be notified, so instead, after the room was freshened up, they left the room keys and a tip for the maid on the dresser then left.

It was late evening when the two men drove past the Polonium 210 operation in a different rented car. The building wasn't that impressive, but they both knew with the amount of money being transacted in this operation, they would probably have very high tech security systems in place, plus a security force.

Rene and Boris agreed they didn't have the time or desire to get clever and try to neutralize the security system, especially when the old ways usually get the job done. Besides, they wanted to do something that would be noticed by the media or as they put it, Shake the shit out of the bushes and see what runs out.

After parking the car two blocks from the site, Boris and Rene took up positions so they could observe the entrance without being detected by the concealed security cameras at the house.

Rene was in total agreement with their plan, but since they had some time on their hands, there wasn't any reason why he shouldn't stir things up a little. "So, Boris, don't you think this plan is a little crude?"

"Do you want to pull back and plan again?" Boris inquired.

"No, no, now that we're here, we may as well stay," was the reply and Boris realized he was not serious, but was rather going to twist his horns again!

After a pause, Rene said, "It reminds me of the cold war days and it does have Soviet Union crude written all over it."

"We got the job done," Boris defended. "Of course, it wasn't pretty like our advisories operations. I think Intelligence in the west watched Hollywood pictures too much. Especially French Intelligence."

"Bolshevik," was the reply.

"Frog," was the counter.

Knowing who the main players were, they waited until most were inside then the two wished each other luck. Boris moved away and disappeared into the shadows. Rene held his position until he saw smoke coming up from behind the house. After raising the collar on his coat and pulling his hat down low over his eyes to hide his identity from the cameras, he walked down the street toward the house. *The old ways still do work,* he thought to himself, as he pretended to brace against the cold while walking. As he approached the house, he could hear shouts. "Fire, fire!" He quickly took up a position by the front door and clicked off the safety on the automatic weapon he had concealed inside his long coat. Having cut the bottom out of his right coat pocket, it allowed him to hold the weapon and he just needed to raise it from under the coat before firing.

The first man out of the house Rene identified as a probable security and didn't take any action, but then the main players started scrambling out. He raised the automatic weapon and starting with the security man, took out the main players. There were security and other people still trying to get out, but paused when they saw the others lying in the street. He didn't care about them and was already taking his planned route of escape.

While running down the street, Rene kept looking back for anyone that might run out of the house and pursue or fire at him. When the people in the house got bunched up inside the front door, they all decided to make a break for it and burst out of the house. Rene was almost to the corner of the street when he saw them, stopped, turned around, but did not fire. His mission was completed and these people were just escaping from the fire, but there was always that ten percent in every crowd, and one of the security people started to fire in Rene's direction. He knelt down and returned fire, but aimed over their heads. A second after he started, Boris opened fire from the opposite corner. With rounds whizzing over their heads and hitting the house, everyone hit the ground and decided not to return fire.

Not hesitating when that occurred, Rene stood and ran over to join Boris who kept the group's attention with additional firing. Once together, the two then moved quickly down the street to an alley, the first part of their planned escape, and they were gone.

CHAPTER 9

One day had passed since the German unit had gotten the word to watch for any unusual movements. It was Pru's turn to watch and once again had the powerful scope focused on their lead's house.

"I say, this chap seems to be handing over airline tickets," he announced.

Met was quick to the scope and after making a minor focus adjustment, agreed they were airline tickets. "I guess we can consider that unusual movement."

Everyone at home base was sitting and talking in their OP center when Bean started reading an incoming message from the German unit. All conversations stopped and everyone had focused on Bean, when Panda then Benz started getting incoming messages as well. The text messages were short, but to the point, and while Blue Jay watched for anything from Italy, the three men decoded their messages.

When JC saw all of the messages were decoded, he inquired, "Anything to report?"

Bean spoke first. "Germany reported seeing airline tickets at the lead's house, but at this time, cannot confirm destination."

"France also reported movement," Panda spoke next, "and Genova, Italy was their destination," followed by Benz with the same destination from the Spain unit.

Since everyone was present, JC called a planning session and walked over to the maps they had hung on the wall. As he looked at the map of Italy, he started to speak. "It looks to me like the terrorists found out their source of Polonium 210 went out of business, have decided to consolidate what they already had, and will move it using the yacht at Sovona Port." JC finished with his right forefinger on Genova and his left on Sovona Port. "The question is should we put everyone into motion?" JC then asked the group.

After discussing the pros and cons, it was decided to put everyone into motion and coded messages were sent out. The units couldn't waste any time getting into position, but by leaving now, should have a head start on the terrorists.

JJ and Mac would man communications at home base while JC and the two home base units flew to Genova.

Everything was already packed including hazmat gear in case the Polonium 210 had to be handled and within an hour JC, Blue Jay, Bean, Benz, and Panda were en route to the airport.

Once they arrived, JC went to file his flight plan and the other men headed straight for the smaller Lear jet and went onboard. A short time later, JC joined them, performed a preflight check, and was ready for takeoff. After communications with the tower, he taxied into position for takeoff and seconds later, the jet was speeding down the runway and lifted into the air. Since the Al-Qaeda people probably weren't on the move yet, the Lear jet would arrive at Genova in plenty of time to get prepared.

———————

Except for Italy, the units were on the move. They would all be using commercial airlines leaving their vehicles at the airport's long-term parking. Their weapons were concealed in the cars and they would get replacements after they reached their destination.

———————

The Lear jet landed at Genova airport, had been directed by the tower to a parking space, and the aircraft was shutdown.

JC and the others stayed on the plane going over plans for the upcoming events. The units were still reporting in to their contacts while they scrambled to get into position. "Are any of the units experiencing any difficulties?" JC inquired.

Each man felt the unit reporting back to him would get into place in time, but Benz expressed concern about the distance the Spain unit would have to travel.

"I agree with your concern," JC acknowledged. "We'll hold off as long as possible, but if they can't get into position, we'll have to execute without their involvement."

After going over additional items and a check of their new porcelain handguns, the five men made their way to the main terminal.

Before getting to the terminal building, the five men split up. The two units went to retrieve the two vehicles that were arranged for them while JC continued on looking for some friendly faces.

JC entered the building, scanned the entire area, discovered what he was looking for, and headed straight for a cocktail lounge across the concourse. It was a small room with a standing room bar in front for those people who were waiting and those not thrilled about flying. JC took a spot at the bar, ordered a scotch on the rocks, and casually looked around. When his drink arrived, he remarked to the bartender as he picked up his drink, "I'm not crazy about flying." He quickly drank the scotch and after paying for the drink moved on.

Shortly after he departed, the man standing to his right also left. After a few minutes, a man at the bar inquired, "Could you tell me where the restrooms are located?" and after getting directions from the bartender, Doggie also left the bar. The three men delayed leaving the restroom until they were the only ones present, then quickly shared information.

Jar Head started with, "We checked all of the incoming flights from Germany, Spain, and France and have narrowed it down to these airlines," he said, showing JC three separate lists of incoming flights that included airlines, times, and gate numbers.

After it was decided, JC would check flights from France, Doggie Spain, and Jar Head Germany, Doggie said, "Checked with Swabbie a short time ago and all was quiet at the yacht. He will notify us if he sees any activity," Doggie added, as he handed a disposable cell phone to JC.

"To review," JC said, "by now, the two units should be in place outside. Since we have three incoming flights and only two units, we will form the required extra unit. When we ID these people, we'll stay with them and notify our people to get into place.

"After they leave the air terminal building and one of the units is on them, we'll pick up your vehicle and become the extra unit.

"After the other two units have dealt with the first two cells that arrive and secure any 210, they will fall back to the yacht area and join Line Backer.

"Hopefully, all of our other units will be in place before we have to take any action," JC added as a final note.

Their meeting completed, the three men spaced out their departures from the restroom, proceeded to the location of the first incoming flight on their list, and waited. They all had studied pictures of all the terrorist cells to great lengths and were confident they would be able to identify them at first sight.

———————

Two of the terrorist cells were on schedule, but the one from France, who should have arrived first, was experiencing delays at Stasbourg International Airport.

———————

After some really fast moving, the units were getting into position. Pru and Met maneuvered slowly along a row of small houses, found two good spots, and held position.

Bris and Jockey moved very cautiously along a back street and located themselves in the darkness.

Check and Tic finally got into position, were playing the parts of two lost bicyclists as their cover, and held position at an off-street location.

Benz notified JC the last unit was in place and the waiting continued.

Two hours had passed and the three men kept checking arrivals from France, Spain, and Germany. After they were satisfied all of the people that deplaned were not the people they were looking for, they proceeded to the gate of the next arrival on their list.

Jar Head sat waiting for people to deplane from the latest arrival from Germany and as he surveyed the area, he started to wonder if he had somehow missed the terrorist when one of the men from the photos they had all committed to memory emerged from the hall leading from the plane. Jar Head remained calm, but his heart rate did increase a little, especially when he realized the next man out of the tunnel was also in one of the photos.

After making sure he got a look at the remaining people that deplaned, and at the same time keeping track of the two he recognized, Jar Head slowly followed. When he figured they were heading for the luggage claim area, he was on his cell phone. "Hello, Uncle Franz," he started. "I must have missed Aunt Freda. I'm going to check the baggage claim area. Maybe she is there."

"You're a good lad, Fritz," Benz commended.

"Thank you, Uncle. I'll get back to you."

Jar Head kept the two in view as Panda and Benz took up a position outside the baggage claim exit.

After grabbing their luggage from the conveyer belt, the two men went out the exit and Jar Head followed. Benz spotted him then quickly looked at the area in front when the cell rang. "Hello again, Uncle. Did you say she would be wearing a blue or brown coat?" was the inquiry and descriptions of the coats the two terrorists were wearing. Benz scanned for a blue and brown coat walking together, found them, then replied, "Aunt Freda called and said she took a bus."

"Okay," was the one-word reply as Jar Head saw the two terrorists board a courtesy bus to the rent-a-car lot and knew the unit had things under control.

Back to the bat cave, he thought smiling to himself, referring to forming the third unit.

Doggie was the next to get a strike when the last two men from the Madrid flight deplaned. Doggie followed pretty much the same procedure as Jar Head except he called his uncle about Aunt Maria.

After turning his two over to Bean and Blue Jay, he went to the parking area and joined Jar Head already waiting in the car.

Due to security and cameras, both units thought it better to wait until their assignments were off airport grounds before they took action. It had to be quick and deadly so the terrorists wouldn't have a chance to communicate with anyone. The units knew how to get it done, but there was just too much activity on airport grounds to guarantee a successful outcome.

Time seemed to be creeping past for the units waiting for the two terrorist cells to clear airport grounds and the third unit waiting for the remaining flight on the list from France to arrive.

The activity at the terminal had slowed down considerably as less and less people were in the terminal building. JC was sipping on his fourth cup of coffee when the flight from Strasbourg, France finally started to deplane. As the people filed out of the hallway, JC recognized the fifth and sixth men in the line as the terrorist cell from France. One was calm and collected, but the other seemed anxious and tense. *That squirrel may prove to be a problem,* JC thought to himself, referring to the anxious man and the almost empty terminal.

Everyone from the flight was heading toward the baggage reclaim area, but when they all followed the signs to baggage claim and the two cell members proceeded to the main entrance, it made JC's job a lot harder.

When the end of the crowd turned off to the left, JC continued walking straight, and after a few more steps, JC pretended he got a call on his cell phone, stopped, and retrieved it from his inside coat pocket. Opening it up, he said, "Hello," and pretended to start a conversation. He began to make gesturers with his arm and hand as if he were getting directions on how to locate someone at the airport. He hoped this would put squirrelly more at ease and as he turned away from the two men, pressed a button on his cell phone.

"Bat cave," Jar Head answered.

"Very funny," JC answered then added, "I'll be at the main entrance shortly. Are you planning to be there?" he continued with the humorous conversation.

"I'm a last minute replacement driver," Jar Head confessed. "Can you describe what you are wearing so I don't pick up the wrong person?"

He obliged by giving him a brief description of the other two men as he again started moving toward the main entrance.

JC was now following at a much greater distance, but the squirrel still kept looking back at him and even got the other man to take a look.

When the two men were going out the exit, JC was just entering the concourse and was again on his cell phone. "I'm about to leave the terminal building. Are you at the airport yet?" he inquired.

"Yes, sir," Jar Head answered. "Parked outside and waiting."

"Good," JC replied and hung up.

The terrorist cell from France was standing just outside the exit when a dark green Mercedes pulled up to the curb, stopped, the two men got into the back seat, and the car sped off.

JC's cell was vibrating and he quickly answered. "Hello," he said, pretending it was a social call.

"I'm illegally parked out here. Can you speed it up a little?" Jar Head requested, due to the quick departure of the Mercedes.

"Almost there," JC assured him.

"Just take your time, but hurry up," Jar Head replied, reminding him not to bring any unnecessary attention from other people or security cameras.

When JC got outside, his ride was parked about ten yards from the curb. He stepped off the curb, moved to the car, and got into the back seat.

When the door slammed closed, Doggie departed at a respectable speed as Jar Head handed JC a weapon.

"Since these two had no luggage, it's a good guess the one with the briefcase would be carrying the Polonium 210. He seemed calm and collected," JC started. "The other one, due to the situation or by nature is a little squirrelly."

"So we have one cool customer that is probably very dangerous, a nut job that will probably go bullshit at the first sign of danger, plus the driver who by now has supplied them with weapons," Doggie summarized the situation.

"That's about it," JC agreed.

"Since a car was sent for these two, I'd say one or both were a little higher up the food chain than the people from Germany and Spain," Jar Head observed. "That means the driver is also their security, well armed, and will have to be taken out first."

"Okay," Doggie said then added, "As in *OK Corral.*"

"Sort of looks that way, Doggie me boy," Jar Head agreed, as he removed his porcelain automatic from its holster, removed the magazine, and cleared the weapon of the round in the chamber. After inserting the cleared round into the mag, he went into a briefcase on the floor and removed another mag containing Teflon tipped rounds, inserted it into the handle of the weapon, and pressed on the slide release allowing it to slam home, putting a round into the chamber in the process.

"Are you all right with this?" Doggie inquired to JC, referring to how they would probably have to handle the situation.

"I agree," JC replied, "but I prefer using Moving Simplicity instead of Cowboy when referring to these types of tactics."

"Moving Simplicity," Doggie echoed, as he and Jar Head smiled remembering what JC had named the quickly organized rescue plan on Corsica.

"We have checked out just about every possible route from the airport to the yacht since we've been here," Doggie was again speaking. "We originally thought the best place should be something rural, but with this guy driving, have a feeling we should look for any opportunity."

The Mercedes didn't make any detours or do something to try to detect anyone following. That was a good thing because in a situation like this, it was hard to maintain a one-car tail without being detected. It also told the third unit the driver was not that good as a security man or that he was overconfident and in this case, being overconfident was worse for him.

They passed through a series of towns that were part of the Italian Riviera and no opportunity had presented itself.

"I guess we'll have to make something happen," Doggie observed, as they approached a remote area between two of the towns.

"Are you thinking about a mile ahead?" Jar Head inquired, and got a yes reply.

"We're talking about a pullover area up ahead," Jar Head informed JC. "It is a remote area and it will give us an opportunity to take the activity off the road. That car may be armored so Doggie and I will go for the driver first while you concentrate on the two in the back."

"Okay," JC agreed, as he clicked off the safety on his 9mm.

Doggie started to close the gap between the two vehicles and as the two cars approached the area of the pullover, he started blowing the horn as Jar Head took a drink out of an empty bottle of Canadian Club whisky. As they got closer to the pullover, Doggie pulled up alongside and kept pace with the Mercedes while Jar Head hung out the window, and offered the other car a drink of whisky out of the bottle.

"Drunken bastards," the driver muttered, as he became uneasy about their driving.

As they approached the pullover, Doggie continued to pass the other car then changed into the other lane too soon, cutting off the other vehicle and both cars went into the pullover area. As Doggie entered the soft dirt, he pressed the accelerator to the floor and spun the wheel to the left, a technique known as, "stab it and steer." His vehicle responded as it started performing a 360-degree turn while the other car slid to a stop in a straight line.

When Doggie let off the gas, the car stopped with the right side facing the Mercedes. Jar Head and JC were out in a flash heading toward the other car with Doggie in hot pursuit. As Jar Head approached, he started firing at the driver and found his thoughts about the car being armored were correct. The rounds made the bullet resistant glass spider web, but they didn't penetrate it.

When JC got to the car, the calm and collected member of the two had a gun in hand, but realized the glass was bullet resistant and didn't fire. What really bothered JC was the cell phone he was holding up to his ear with the other hand and started firing pointblank at the rear window. The man turned away a little but kept his cool. With three guns now firing at the car, the squirrel went bullshit, grabbed the briefcase, and bailed out the other door.

JC saw this, knew the 210 was probably in the case, and started moving around the car to give chase at the same time alerting the other two.

The glass was real good, but could not stand up to so much punishment and the rounds finally passed through killing the driver and after exchanging a few rounds with the man in the back seat, he was dead too.

The man with the briefcase was running toward the woods just beyond the turnoff when he suddenly stopped, opened the briefcase, and yelled, "I'll set it off," probably referring to some sort of booby-trap device attached to the Polonium 210.

JC came to an abrupt halt with his weapon at the ready and mumbled, "Set this off, squirrel food," as he squeezed off a round that struck the man between the eyes killing him instantly.

"This is just a guess mind you, but I don't think the man hesitates," Jar Head offered an opinion to Doggie.

"And we're all still here," Doggie added, as they both shook their heads and went to get the hazmat gear before they retrieved the Polonium 210.

He was sure the man was dead, but approached to make sure. Once satisfied, he took out his cell phone and called Line Backer. "Things went well, but the competition made a call, probably to his parent company and a counteroffer may be coming," JC said, informing them the terrorist may have gotten a call out.

"We planned for that eventually and are ready with another offer," Swabbie assured JC, confirming he would alert all units.

"Good," he answered, "see you soon." He hung up as his two partners approached with the gear to move the Polonium 210 safely.

———————

With the Polonium 210 safely in tow, everyone loaded into their vehicles, took separate routes back to the airport, and the waiting Lear jet.

Doggie, Swabbie, and Jar Head would take the car they had been using since they got there and were the last to leave, but before they left, Jar Head took a throwaway cell phone out of his pocket and said, "I guess it's that time?"

While he dialed a number they shouldn't have had, his two partners were focusing in on the yacht with field glasses. On the third ring, someone on the bridge answered and Jar Head started talking in Italian. The man that answered the phone didn't speak the language and didn't know what to do, so he handed it to a well-dressed man standing next to him. Jar Head again spoke in Italian until the man started interrupting. "You no speak Italiano? How about English?" he asked in a very convincing manner.

"Yes, English," the man agreed.

"I have a message for you boss," Jar Head said. "We don't like what you are doing in our country, so take it somewhere else."

"Who is this?" the man on the phone demanded.

"Never mind who it is. Just know if you don't leave or if you ever come back, you will stay here permanently."

"Is that a threat?" the man again demanded.

"Threat, promise, whatever you like," Jar Head said and hung up.

"Oh, you got their attention," Doggie relayed. "Their mouths, arms, and hands are moving all over the place."

"I'll say," Swabbie agreed, "now let's get."

"So do we have to call you Marlin from now on?" Doggie asked.

"Not all of the time, but once in a while would be nice," Jar Head replied.

The man in the back seat of the Mercedes did get a call out to his terrorist cell and they had decided to leave that site and set up in another part of France. They scrambled around packing some things, burning others, and constantly talked about how they would make the world pay.

When the terrorist cell was ready to leave, the new self-appointed leader stopped everyone just prior to going out the door and said, "We were almost successful this time, but next time we must not fail. Now we will disperse, but very soon we will regroup and make them all pay for killing our brothers." After getting approval of his words from the group, the man felt he was indeed the new cell leader. The former leader was bad, but this man was evil itself. He was one of those people that didn't really believe in any cause, just enjoyed the death and destruction these latest terrorist activities brought to the world. He was almost gleeful as he opened the door and 9mm rounds came flying in. Mr. Gleeful and the man next to him were the first to be cut down and the remaining quickly followed.

As the room was checked for any documents with valuable information, one of the men inquired, "I say, wonder how many cells like this are active in France?"

"Good question. It seems to be coming into vogue everywhere," Met answered.

"Well, there should be a few less after today," Pru stated, as Jockey and Bris picked the lock on the back door of a hotel outside of Madrid, Spain around the same time

Check and Tic rode their bikes down a long lane to a house in Stuttgart, Germany.

The Lear Jet held position at Genova Airport in case the other units had trouble. If that occurred, they would fly to that country to assist. If more than one unit had a problem, the jet would land, one of the reserve units would deplane, and the Lear Jet would continue onto the next country. It was not the best of plans, but with limited manpower it was the best one could do. Besides, the Team had become very close and if the opposition got in the way of a rescue party, they would pay a heavy price if they didn't back off.

When all of the units reported in the Lear Jet taxied for takeoff and the trip back to Luxembourg knowing everything had gone off as planned.

During the planning stage, concerns about the units that were originally in place and known by the locals suddenly disappearing after the terrorists were eliminated. In a situation like that, the local people would be more apt to report them to the authorities during the investigation.

To get around that, a very ambitious plan of rotating the units was developed. The original unit in a country would supply information, leave transportation and weapons at the airport's long-term parking. The incoming unit would take out the terrorist cell then leave without making any contact with the locals.

CHAPTER 10

A few days had passed since Project completion and everyone was at the forward home base enjoying a second cup of coffee after morning breakfast.

"Another fine job," JJ commended everyone then seemed to go into deep thought.

"What's on your mind?" Mac inquired.

"I was just wondering who was connected to that yacht," JJ replied.

"Think we could find out from the source that told us about it in the first place?" Mac asked.

"They either don't know or they wouldn't say," JJ answered.

"Think they are still in Savona?" Mac wondered.

"No," Jar Head answered and everyone just figured he was expressing an opinion or almost everyone.

Blue Jay looked at Bean and flipped his eyes toward the ceiling and Bean said in a low voice, "Can hardly wait for this one." Both knew Jar Head didn't answer a question of that sort unless he knew the answer.

"If they did leave, I'd love to know their destination," JJ again spoke.

"Oh, they left all right," Doggie assured him. "Jar Head made a little phone call before we left, led them to believe he was from a local group of concerned citizens, and told them they better leave."

"And you think that scared them off?" Mac inquired.

"Either that or they were ordered by their boss to leave," Jar Head assured him.

"Here it comes, whatever it is," Blue Jay whispered.

"That's all well and good if your guesswork is correct, but unless you have a crystal ball…" JJ observed.

"Swabbie, look into the crystal ball and tell him where the yacht is," Jar Head instructed.

"Just sort of wandering around in the Mediterranean Sea right now. Would you like the general area?" Swabbie inquired.

"This is all very amusing…" JJ started when Doggie interrupted with, "Swabbie, give him the general area."

"Sort of wandering around between Nice, France, and the island of Corsica," Swabbie answered.

Before anyone could respond, Benz, who was sitting next to him, inquired with a smile, "How did you get that thing rigged up?"

"We just thought it might come in handy and since we had some time on our hands…" Swabbie explained.

After everyone heard the question and answer, they all moved around Swabbie who brought both hands up to table level showing a device displaying coordinates on its little screen.

"Okay, what is it?" JJ inquired, as JC and the others chuckled.

"There is a GPS type product they sell on the open market so parents can keep track of their kids. Well, this is the super duper version that we probably shouldn't even have in our possession, but that's another story," Swabbie explained.

"How did you get it onto the yacht?" JJ asked.

"Flipper did it," Swabbie informed him, as he motioned toward Doggie who immediately said, "I!" as he raised his right hand. "Back in the day, I was in special units, Para scuba and stuff," Doggie explained. "While two other people created a diversion, I was able to hook the yacht up with the sending end of that gizmo, it bounces off a satellite, and down into that end."

"How about if it stops working or malfunctions?" Mac inquired.

"It's onto plan B if it works," Doggie assured him.

"And plan B is," Mac pursued.

"This," Doggie replied, as he produced another unit he had in his lap, said, "Plan B still works."

"I knew he was going to do something like that," JC said, as he burst into laughter.

"And how did you know that?" Mac asked.

"Because we are all part of the brotherhood," JC explained.

"What brotherhood?" Mac inquired.

"The Brotherhood of the Floating Simplicity," JC said, as he pushed Mac's shoulder.

"Not that shit again. I almost went to see the talking doctor after that last episode of, The Floating Simplicity," Mac said with a smile.

As the group continued talking about the devices, JJ was already thinking about the next step. Everyone would be leaving Luxembourg that afternoon and flying back to New Jersey. En route, he would schedule a meeting of the Board for first thing the next morning to brief them on the Project, and then bring them up to date on this new revelation.

At the very least, they should keep track of where the yacht would go or maybe turn it over to their source in the Intelligence Community.

JJ was able to contact each Board member from the plane and all were in attendance when he called the meeting to order.

Since Dunn brought the Project to the Board and his sources were the ones in the Republic of Georgia, JJ asked him to present first.

Gil had completed his part of the briefing and after a series of questions; JJ again had the floor. "Thank you Gil, very impressive," he started, "and a special thank you to your sources, whoever they are."

"I would relay the message, but they don't know about you or the Board either," Dunn replied.

Everyone smiled at the remarks knowing security and on a need to know basis were an absolute must for this type of work.

After JJ complimented Dunn and his sources, he presented the Team's part of the Project. The first concerns of the Board were the well being of the Team members. After JJ assured them all were well, they moved onto a series of questions about the Project itself.

With no more questions being asked, JJ moved onto the new revelations and soon had the Board members sitting up straight in their seats.

He had presented all of the information about the yacht then said, "As you know, this was not part of the Project, but I personally feel we just can't sit on this information, even if it is turned over to the Intelligence Community for them to deal with.

"That completes my portion of the briefing. I feel we should start discussing what to do about the yacht," JJ finished.

"Your suggestion about turning it over to the Intelligence Community could turn out to be a catch 22," Dunn started. "Just for conversation, let's say we gave it to a source within US Intel. The source couldn't reveal the Project or say it came from us, so they would pass it off as a very confidential contact and that would get by until one of their superiors asked for the identity of the contact. Since we are talking about a yacht, that to them just seems to be sailing around, they will ask that question. Can tell you I would have when serving as DDO. Now the source is in a corner. They either give us up or lie and if you lie, it has to be something that will stand up under intense scrutiny."

"So if it's not turned over to US Intel, the remaining options are use the Team if we decide there is a real need or just track them for information purposes?" Mr. Howard inquired.

"Well, yes, yes and maybe," Admiral Fox spoke up. "At this point, we are not sure where they are going. If Italy was a failed mission, they might just return to their homeport and we may get an idea of who was involved.

"However, the Project did cut off their source of Polonium 210 and maybe the Team just intercepted the final shipments. If that is the case, they may have a shitload of the stuff. We have interrupted their plans and higher ups are deciding on their next move.

"So, yes, I suggest we watch to see what they do. Yes, use the Team if it is absolutely necessary. I say absolutely necessary because under normal circumstances, it would be too soon to send them out again, especially after they just completed such a difficult Project. Maybe turn it over to US Intel if needed, but Gil made an excellent point about a catch 22. We should try to find a way around that."

"Any other ideas?" JJ asked everyone. When no one spoke up, he said, "Well, all of your points are well-taken and we would need a way around the catch 22. Gil, you are the logical choice for finding a way around it in case we need US Intel involvement."

Gil had no problem with that and agreed.

"I see this matter will require a lot of discussion so maybe we should break for coffee at this time," JJ suggested.

As the Board broke for coffee, Mac said, "Very good analysis, Admiral Fox," then added, "for a sailor."

"I'm surprised you were able to recognize good analysis, General Mac," he replied. "I thought anything besides charging up a hill with a bayonet in your teeth was beyond you, ya fucking Marine."

"Now, Foxie, don't get tense," Mac said to one of his lifelong friends as they both chuckled.

The Board meeting continued for several more hours. One thing about this group, if they see a real need to deal with something, they don't give up until they are all satisfied.

After a while, JJ felt the meeting had gone on long enough for one day and suggested, "Gentlemen, it has been a long day. Maybe we should get a fresh start in the morning, but there is one item we have to decide on right now. Should we ask the Team to delay leaving for their after Project furloughs until the yacht issue is resolved?"

After some additional discussion, the Board agreed the Team should be asked to delay furloughs if possible.

———————

The following morning, JJ and Mac went looking for JC to discuss the delayed furloughs. Not finding him or anyone else in the main area of the Barn, they then looked in the Como shop with the same result. "Maybe they all went out for a run," JJ reasoned.

"Maybe they already started furloughs," Mac quipped.

The two then checked the Team meeting room and found everyone was there including Jar Head, Doggie, and Swabbie. "So you're all here keeping track of the yacht?" JJ remarked.

"Well, that plus developing some contingency plans," JC replied. "Yesterday, when you were meeting with the Board, we all got together to discuss the yacht situation and decided to stay until it was somehow resolved."

"The Team and Board seem to be on the same page," JJ remarked. "That's what Mac and I came to discuss with all of you. Mind if we sit in?" he asked.

"Would appreciate it," JC said then added, "And maybe you could brief us on what the Board's feelings are about the yacht?"

"Good idea," JJ agreed, as he went to the front of the room.

After JJ had brought the Team up to date, JC said, "Now let me bring you and Mac up to date on our thoughts," he said, pointing to a chalkboard behind him. "We have what amounts to a bunch of what ifs or some might call it a logic diagram. If the yacht has no 210 it may just be wandering around so it doesn't lead anyone back to its homeport. If it does have 210 onboard, the question is what are their plans for it? Deliver it to someone developing a nuclear bomb, disperse it around the world to other terrorist groups, or maybe just sail into a busy harbor and explode the yacht sending the radioactive material everywhere."

"That's where we are and as you can see, have subcategories under each," JC concluded.

"May have another subcategory for busy harbor," Bean spoke up. "We have been focusing on commercial shipping, but who and what are the main targets of terrorism: the people and the media. If they target commercial ships, they could contaminate ships at dock and affect workers on the ships and dock. Now keeping in mind their main targets, how about if they pick a day when a lot of cruise ships are in a certain harbor and in the process of unloading or loading passengers? They ram a large cruise ship then set off explosives they have stored onboard. With the amount of explosives they could store on a vessel of that size, they would probably sink the ship at the dock. Those cruise ships are huge, but remember what a very small boat did to the USS Cole.

"As for the 210 there is usually a seabreeze coming in off the ocean during the day and it could spread over a wider area inland.

"In that type of atmosphere, it would affect thousands of people and create a media frenzy," Bean finished.

"You and Mr. Black have a lot in common," Mac observed. "You have a way of fucking up a perfectly good day," He said, referring to the topic of great concern Bean had just presented.

"Who is Mr. Black?" Swabbie whispered to JJ.

"That's Gil's codename," JJ replied.

"Good one," JC acknowledged to Bean, as he started to write the new subcategory on the board then stopped and turned around. "You are happy with us here aren't you?" he inquired, referring to the terrorist plan Bean just rolled out. "Maybe more money or something? We don't want you getting pissed off and going over."

"If you're going to fight them, sometimes you have to think like them," Bean announced, as the Team chuckled at the exchanges.

"Just checking," JC said with a smile, as he continued writing on the board.

The group continued their informal meeting and when they got to Bean's new entry decided to break for lunch knowing it would probably take up most of the afternoon.

As everyone stood and started filling out of the meeting room, Panda inquired, "So do you think Beanie Weenie will be going over to the other side anytime soon?"

"Well, first of all, it isn't Beanie Weenie," Blue Jay scolded, "it's Beanie *the* Weenie."

"Oh, is that what it is? Well, all birds have a beak so maybe we should call you peckerface," Bean fired back then added, "and your entire head looks like a pecker," as he looked at Panda.

"Was it something we said?" Panda laughed, as he pleaded to Blue Jay.

"It's all Mac's fault," he answered. "If he had put in those PMS vending machines like he promised, we wouldn't have these outbursts."

"You ladies keep me out of your little squabbles," Mac's voice pleaded from the back of the group.

"It's good to see our sons have found some playmates," Jar Head said to Doggie, as both enjoyed the verbal combat.

Taking their usual mealtime route, the group was passing through the kitchen when Jockey inquired, "So, Top, will you be cooking today?"

"Who else?" Top replied, knowing that was probably the first shot of another verbal ambush.

"As you know, Top is our resident chef," Jockey addressed his remarks to Jar Head, Doggie, and Swabbie. "But you may not know that Top is an avid admirer of Emeril; watches his TV show daily and will soon have a show of his own on the Food Network. I know, was surprised myself." He continued. "It will be called Top's Slop and will air every afternoon."

At this point, Top usually took some sort of retaliatory action, but this time he didn't say anything which surprised everyone, especially Jockey.

"Nothing to say?" Jockey inquired.

"Not today," Top replied then continued with, "Good afternoon, gentlemen. Today we will be having Flemish Stew for lunch. Was planning to serve it family style, but have changed my mind and it will served à la carte." Then he looked at Jockey and said, "And yours will have the real deal in it." Then cleared his throat.

"Holy shit," one of the Team members commented and everyone burst into laughter.

"I have twenty dollars for anyone that wants to trade plates," Jockey announced.

"Wouldn't if I were you," Top warned everyone, as he shook his head no.

When everyone left the kitchen, Top and the Ladies started to laugh. "We should start videotaping these little skirmishes between you and Jockey," LadyA suggested and the other two agreed as they continued laughing.

After a noisy lunch, everyone returned to the Team' meeting room and started to discuss Bean's new entry.

It was late afternoon when Swabbie stood and walked over to a map of the Mediterranean Sea that was hung on the wall so the yacht's movements could be tracked.

After finding the coordinates on the map that were displayed on the device, he made a mark on the map of the yacht's position, then drew a line from the previous make he made to this one. "Somebody may have made a decision," Swabbie announced and everyone gathered around the map.

"Any ideas about where they may be heading?" JJ inquired.

"Well," Swabbie started his reply, "after they departed Savona Port, they went into the Mediterranean and sort of wandered around, but the last three times I checked, it looked like they may have set a course and if we line up on these last three marks," he said, as he extended a briefing pointer and laid it across the marks on the map, "they may be heading for Spain, Morocco, Algeria, or out of the Med altogether."

"If they left the Med and turned south, they would probably be heading for a friendly port," Mac spoke up, as he gestured toward the map. If north, they could be targeting France or more likely the UK, but if they continued on a straight course, the next stop could be the US."

"I guess we should get everyone on the Board up to date and kick that plan to alert the Intelligence community into high gear," Mac added, as he looked at JJ who shook his head in agreement.

CHAPTER 11

Swabbie, Doggie, and Jar Head kept watch day and night on the yacht's progress. It did change course once and made port in Algeria, probably for fuel, but then continued on its original course.

It looked like it would be leaving the Mediterranean Sea the following day and JJ decided it best the Board was in session. If the yacht turned left, they would just monitor its progress. If right or straight, they would take appropriate action.

JJ and the Board were in session when his cell phone rang. He excused himself and answered. "Hello."

"Just giving you a heads up on that stock I was telling you about. Looks like it is going straight to the top."

"Thank you for the information," JJ said and hung up.

"Looks like the yacht may be coming our way," he informed everyone.

The Board had already discussed this situation in great length and decisions were already made for every possible situation they could think of. It was now just a matter of finalizing on their course of action. "Since it looks like the yacht may be heading for the US, are we all still in agreement about informing the Intelligence Community?" JJ inquired. All agreed. "Gil, I guess it's a go for US Intel," JJ informed Dunn.

"It's good our decision was already made about this," Gil replied. "It will save some time and I have a feeling time may turn out to be our worst enemy."

"Will you require any help from us?" JJ inquired.

"Not at this time, but that may change," Dunn answered then added, "However, I was wondering if Foxie had any connections that could locate a Naval Officer that served in the Mediterranean back in 1993."

"I could do that," a puzzled Foxie replied.

Seeing the look, Gil quickly added, "Just an idea for contingency planning we can all kick around."

––––––––––––––

Dunn had already been in touch with Di Flippi, one of his close friends, and a subordinate from his days at CIA and was heading for their first meeting about this topic. Through an encrypted phone conversation from Dunn, Di Flippi knew he wanted to meet and the location would be at the starting point of Pickett's Charge in Gettysburg National Park.

I'll bet Di Flippi was surprised when he got the call instead of the other way around. Gil thought about past calls from Di that turned into Projects for the Board and Team. Dunn knew it was going to be difficult for Di Flippi to get everyone's attention about the yacht without supplying them with the identity of a good source the information came from, preferably not him and the Board.

Dunn passed through the town of Gettysburg, entered the park, and headed for the meeting point. Since he came from Virginia and had a shorter drive, Gil wasn't surprised when he saw Di had already arrived. Parking a short distance from the other car, Dunn got out and walked into the wooded area that overlooked the fields where Pickett's Division had made their attack over 144 years ago.

Di Flippi was standing at the edge of the woods as Gil approached. "Just trying to imagine how it must have been," Di said.

"Old tactics against newer types of warfare," Dunn observed. "Says something about the steel of the men that made the charge doesn't it?"

Di didn't reply as both men continued looking at the fields and that small clump of trees in the distance.

After a few minutes, Gil broke the silence with, "Have one for you this time."

"Nothing good I'll bet," Di Flippi observed. "Any time John's widow comes up in our conversations, it's off to the races."

"This time it's the same thing, only different, maybe," Gil assured him.

"Well, I'm glad we're clear on that point," Di Flippi replied then inquired, "Think it's too late to join the charge?" as he stepped toward the field.

"It may not be that bad," Gil assured.

"The optimum words being *may not,*" Di replied then added, "Prefer *will not.*"

"Let me lay it out for you," Dunn said. "I may even be able to help out."

"How nice," Di Flippi acknowledged, as he took another step toward the field.

As the two men strolled through the woods where Pickett's Division waited prior to their charge, Dunn brought Di Flippi up to date on everything. When he finished, Di made the same observation that Dunn had during the Board meeting. "You know, this could turn into a catch 22 situation, don't you?" and Gil acknowledged with a headshake.

"I have the obvious problem of coming up with a source that would stand up under intense scrutiny, plus have eager beaver political types to deal with that seem to be finding their way into the antiterrorist game at the Agency."

"That is where I may be able to help," Gil offered.

"There you go with that *may be* shit again," Di replied.

"Okay, *will be,*" Dunn corrected, as he shook his head and smiled. "You can't make the source up because it probably would not stand up under scrutiny and you can't give the real source, we hope. How about an anonymous source that would stand up, but would be very difficult to verify?"

"That could work," Di Flippi agreed, "but it would have to be a source that was believable, that I could push, but at the same time be able to maintain deniability about the true identity of the source. This would go up the chain to the top, then over to Defense Department to get the Navy involved."

"At least," was Dunn's two-word reply.

"What do you mean at least?" Di inquired.

"I think my idea will work," Dunn assured him. "As for the yacht itself, we think maybe a prince has too much money on his hands and that means those people at the State Department will get involved."

"I'm not making the charge. Just fucking shoot me right here," Di suggested.

"It shouldn't be that bad," Dunn assured. "With a possible terrorist threat involved, how much could they resist?"

"Know I've said this before, but I'll say it again," Di admitted, "I never liked you."

"Not ever?" Gil asked.

"Not ever," Di confirmed.

The two men continued walking as Dunn rolled out his idea and after a few suggestions from Di Flippi, they called it a plan.

"What about contingency planning?" Di inquired.

"Funny you should ask," Gil smiled.

"Bet I'm not going to like this either," Di surmised.

"May ask you to meet with a man," Gil said. "I would do it myself, but he knows I am no longer at the Agency and it might generate too many questions."

"Who is he?" Di asked.

"You may not remember, but you met him back in 1993. He was the Lieutenant with that SEAL team that we sent to secure a beach area, then transported Jar Head and Doggie out of harm's way."

"I remember him," Di Flippi acknowledged. "You had him come to your office at the Agency to thank him and didn't we ask the Navy to detach him to us a few times after that?"

"That was him," Dunn confirmed. "Have someone trying to locate him for me. After I get the scoop on what he has been doing since then, may ask you to talk with him."

"About…" was the one-word question.

"About that contingency plan you have been bugging me about," Gil answered then continued with the details.

————————

Due to the severity of the situation, JJ and the Board were meeting daily and at the next morning's meeting, Foxie had the information Dunn had requested and during a coffee break brought Dunn up to date. "Here is the scoop on your man," Foxie said, as he opened a folder and put it on the table. "Per his requests, he has spent a lot of time with the Seal Teams since the nineties. Looks to me like he is a natural for that type of duty, but now when he should be with the teams, they have him stuck in supply. He is a Lieutenant Commander and coming up on nineteen years of service. Probably would have a higher rank if he wasn't with the teams so much."

"See problems of any kind?" Gil inquired.

"Not that I can see," Foxie replied, as he again scanned the pages in the folder.

"Where is he currently stationed?" Dunn asked, as he removed a notebook and pen from his inside pocket.

"Norfolk Naval Base in Virginia," Foxie started then continued with the detailed address and a phone number.

When Gil had completed writing down the information, he asked, "This question is probably something you would have no way of knowing, but do you think he could get leave if he requested it?"

"Don't see why not. If he has leave available on the books," Foxie answered. "But if he can't get leave and your reason is important enough, maybe I could arrange to have him assigned to Naval Intel for a while."

"When we reconvene I'm going to run this addition to the contingency plan past everyone for approval."

"Sounds good," Foxie approved.

When JJ called the meeting back to order, Dunn requested the floor and presented his addition to the contingency plan they were working on.

Since the meeting with Dunn at Gettysburg, Di Flippi had been very busy. First, he had prepared for the anonymous tip about the yacht that would be coming through at any time. Dunn had already given him the okay about the SEAL, he had gotten in touch with him, and they would meet that evening in Washington, DC.

Di was at his desk wondering if his surprised look would be convincing when he was given the information about the yacht when one of the people in his unit approached his desk and said, "We may have a situation."

"What is it?" Di inquired, hoping it was the yacht and not a second situation they would have to deal with at the same time.

"An anonymous tip was received about a yacht containing a large amount of Polonium 210 heading for our east coast."

"Did you backtrack the anonymous tip?" Di Flippi inquired.

"Yes, sir," the young man answered. "It came out of France, but we couldn't pinpoint the location. However, this same source in the past has been reliable, but we have never been able to ID it."

"Do we know this yacht exists?" Di then asked.

"It does exist," he confirmed. "Have been in touch with Navy Intel and they have verified it through naval ships in the general area."

"Okay, let's ID this bird," Di ordered. "Request the Navy to do a very high flyby so they don't spook the yacht."

"Yes, sir," the young man answered, as he quickly departed to carry out the order.

I'm impressed, Di thought to himself. *This kid is performing exactly the way he is supposed to plus anticipating and carrying things out on his own. Not bad at all.*

Naval aircraft was already in the area and were just vectored to the area of the yacht's last know location and in no time, the craft was found and identified.

When the information was received at the Agency's OPS center, the craft's name was first verified then past and present ownership were traced plus many more detailed items were checked out.

Since the 9/11 committee pointed out the lack of communication between different agencies, the CIA had been forced to work more closely with and share intelligence with other departments inside the government. One of them was the Intelligence arm of the State Department who had a bad habit of sometimes mixing too much diplomacy with Intelligence work.

Several hours later, Di Flippi and other staff members were going over the information about the ownership of the yacht when one of those State Department types approached his desk. "I want to talk about this yacht situation. Over at State we think you are blowing this out of proportion."

"Why do you say that?" Di inquired.

"Why?" the man jumped. "From an anonymous tip you have the OPS center scrambling around and the Navy tracking that yacht and the worst thing it can be doing is taking those people onboard for a cruise."

"Is that why you are paying us this visit?" Di asked.

"Yes, I feel it is a total waste of resources and manpower," he replied.

"No, that isn't the reason," Di Flippi corrected him. "The real reason is you have seen that one of the previous owners of the yacht is a Saudi prince and you people are again putting diplomacy and politics before Intelligence."

"That's not it at all," the man demanded.

"Well, there's only one other possibility and that is you are an idiot," Di stated.

"We'll see about this," the man from State promised, as he stormed off.

"He seems to have his victory secrets in a bunch today," Di observed, as he continued reviewing the Intel.

The issue did go up the chain, but when the Defense Department agreed with the Agency, State got overruled and plans were put into motion for the Navy to intercept the yacht as it approached the US east coast and conducted a search of the vessel.

CHAPTER 12

The Board never got a chance to do a detailed post review of the last project and were just finalizing on some logistical issues when JJ's phone started to vibrate. He removed it from his pocket opened it, and said, "Hello."

"Your travel agent called and said the vacation cruise you had planned was booked," LadyA informed JJ.

"That's too bad. I was looking forward to it," JJ said then inquired, "Did she offer any alternatives?"

"She did say something about the Bahamas or Jamaica, but wants you to call her," LadyA replied.

"Thank you, I will," JJ said, hung up then told the Board, "The yacht has changed course.

"Are they sure the device is working properly?" Dawson asked.

"Yes," JJ confirmed, "they have a backup in place and I'm sure both were checked and show the same coordinates."

"Could we be wrong about the yacht?" Wilson asked.

We could be, Gil thought to himself, *but I'll put my money on another reason.*

"Let's discuss our course of action," JJ said, calling the meeting back to order.

Dawson was the first to speak. "Let me do a quick review," he started. "We managed indirectly to alert the Intelligence Community about the yacht and they in turn got the Defense Department involved. The yacht was to be stopped and inspected on the high seas. Now all of a sudden the yacht changed course and that tells me one of two things: we were wrong about the yacht in the first place or somebody alerted the yacht."

"Good point," Dunn told Dawson as he stood up. "Give me a few minutes and I'll see what I can find out." Then he left the room.

Gil went down the elevator and left the building. After walking a few blocks, he found a subway entrance, walked down the stairs, and looked for the first available train. He didn't care about its destination, he just wanted to be out of the immediate area and after a few minutes was on an express train heading uptown. After a few stops, he got off the train, went to street level, started walking, removed a throwaway cell phone from his coat pocket, and dialed eleven numbers. On the second ring, Di Flippi's voice said, "Hello."

"Hi, Di," Gil said, not identifying himself. "I just heard a rumor that you won't be able to attend the getaway weekend."

That sounded innocent enough, but Di knew what it meant. "I'm afraid that's true," Di Flippi acknowledged. "Something personal came up."

"It's not the same reason that kept you away back in 93 is it?"

"No, nothing like that," Di admitted. "This actually is something very stupid, but I'd rather not go into it right now."

"No problem," Gil backed off. "The other day, the wife and I were talking about taking a getaway flight to somewhere exotic and she suggested asking you and Gloria to come along. Are you up for that?"

"It sounds real good," Di agreed. "I think it's a good time for us to take a break."

"Think we should tell our friends about it. Don't want them to get mad at us," Gil said.

"That's probably a good idea. I'll get in touch with them," Di agreed.

The two men continued their conversation a little while longer, then Di said he had to get back to work and they hung up.

Gil turned around and started walking back toward the subway as he reviewed the conversation in his head and the question and answer routine he and Di had developed over the years.

"Question: won't be able to attend the getaway weekend. (They aren't stopping the yacht). Answer: I'm afraid that's true, something personal came up. (Di agreed and it was within the Intel community).

Question: It's not the same reason that kept you away back in 93. (In 1993, they discovered a traitor inside the Intel Community). Answer: No, nothing like that. This actually is something very stupid. (No traitor, but someone allowed the opposition to find out about the operation). Question: taking a getaway flight to somewhere exotic and she suggested asking you and Gloria to come along. Are you up for that? (Go with the contingency plan and the SEAL). Answer: It sounds real good. (Agreed).

Question: Think we should tell our friends about it, don't want them to get mad at us. (Notify UK, yacht may make port in their territory). Answer: That's probably a good idea. I'll get in touch with them. (Agreed).

After Di Flippi spoke with Gil, he sat back in his chair and reflected back on the old days at the Agency when a voice jarred him out of his thoughts. "Did you want to see me?" the man from the State Department asked in a very condescending voice.

"Yes, I do, have a seat," Di said, trying not to tie into the snobby bastard.

"I'll stand," he replied.

"I have a question about the yacht situation." Di Flippi cut right to the chase.

"What about it?" he replied. "It changed course. We were right and you were wrong."

"Who are the *we?*" Di inquired.

"What?" the man asked.

"You said *we* were right. I just want to know who your accomplices were," Di questioned. "Are you that stupid that you thought we wouldn't find out about your little communications to Foreign Intelligence organizations about the yacht and how someone warned the yacht to change course?"

"I didn't warn anybody," he defended. "I just did some checking on my own-"

"To Foreign Intelligence agencies that we know are compromised, you pompous ass," Di said, as his voice started to rise. "I'm initiating an investigation into this matter and I'd say the best you can hope for is a gross incompetence charge. Maybe you can get a job with that prince you were trying to protect. Now get the fuck out of here."

After the man departed, Di Flippi sat back in his chair and as members of his staff came into the office, he said, "You know this new sharing of information between US Intelligence is both good and bad. It's good if we are all on the same page working toward the same goal, but over the years, we have always had a problem with State because there are always too many like him."

When Dunn returned to the meeting, the Board was discussing the change of events and courses of action.

Gil quickly went to his seat and started to update the Board members. "For time's sake, I'll give you the short and sweet version," Dunn started. "As we already know, the yacht has changed course. My source said the yacht was warned and probably changed course to avoid being boarded. Don't have the details, but it wasn't intentional. I asked for an opinion about activating our contingency plan and they were in favor of activation."

"Well, if they found out the yacht was warned somehow, wouldn't they just reinitiate their plan?" Howard asked.

"Yes, under normal circumstances they probably would if they found out they were somehow warned off. However, in this situation, the yacht has changed course, is no longer heading toward US shores, and a Saudi prince has been connected to the vessel," Gil answered. "I'll do a little speculation here and say Intelligence and Defense are on one side, State and their diplomats on the other with somebody in the middle trying to make a decision."

With the updated information from Dunn, the Board discussed whether to activate their contingency plans or trust that the government would take action if the yacht again moved toward the US shores.

After a few hours, the Board voted to activate the contingency plans if the situation changed and if it looked like the government could not or would not act quickly enough.

After the morning meeting, JJ and Mac drove back to update everyone concerning the Board's decision and the contingency plans. Instead of stopping at the house, JJ drove up to the Barn and parked by the main entrance. The two men went inside and first went to check the Team's meeting room. "Good," JJ told Mac, "everyone is already assembled." Both men entered the room. JJ asked if he could make an announcement and JC turned the floor over to him.

"Gentlemen," JJ started. "Mac and I just came from a Board meeting and it has been decided not to put the contingency plans into motion unless it becomes obvious to us there is no alternative. We came to this decision for two reasons. One, the terrorists like to make a big statement when they do something. They could do something in the Caribbean, but if they made such a big investment, we feel they would want a bigger target that would create a media frenzy. The second reason is if the yacht turns back toward the US coast, the Navy will intercept and board them. Open to any questions or comments," JJ added.

Bean was the first with a question. "The Board and Team developed a contingency plan and I feel we should at the very least get into position so we can execute it if needed."

"That was considered," JJ answered, "but we didn't see the need at this time."

"Didn't see the need," Bean echoed his words. "Well, what would be considered a need at this time?"

"I think your son is going to be bad," Jar Head whispered to Doggie who whispered back, "That's my boooy."

"Well, let's review the facts in some detail," JJ offered. "The yacht seems to be heading into the Caribbean and we're not sure, but it may be heading for Grand Cayman or Jamaica and for the reasons stated, we don't feel there are big enough targets in those areas."

"Freedom of the Seas," Bean said.

"Yes, I guess you could look at it that way, they can go wherever they like," JJ agreed.

"No," Bean corrected. "Freedom of the Seas as in the world's largest cruise ship with a port of call at Georgetown, Grand Cayman on the fourth day and Montego Bay, Jamaica on the fifth. If I were a terrorist and was forced to change my original plan, this would be my contingence plan. Besides, we all know about Al-Qaeda and the word thing that started with 9/11. In addition to that, the next time Freedom of the Seas pulls into Grand Cayman, eleven other cruise ships will also be there for the day."

"Are you sure about all of this?" JJ inquired.

"It's right here," Bean offered, turning around a laptop he had been using to access sailing dates and other information on the web. "But there's something nagging at me that I can't quite put my finger on."

As JJ and the others scanned the computer's screen, Mac asked JC, "You're sure the kid is happy with us? He's starting to scare me."

"I know," JC agreed, going along with Mac's humor.

"Yes, Uncle Mac and Uncle JC. I'm happy, happy," Bean assured them then started to laugh.

JJ was going through the departure dates and said, "Let's assume the yacht was on schedule to hit the ship while it was taking on passengers at Miami, Florida when it was warned and had to turn away. You're saying their contingency plan may be to lay in wait for them at a port of call. If Bean's reasoning is correct, how do we proceed?"

"I suggest we first set up at Grand Cayman. If the yacht doesn't show up, we'll move onto Montego Bay. We are already very familiar with that area and would be able to set up very quickly," JC offered.

"What makes you think they would pull into port?" Mac asked. "They could stick to what looked like their original plan and just sail in and ram the other ship."

"I don't think they will use that tactic now," JC guessed. "They were warned about being stopped, but the Navy didn't pursue when they changed course. That probably told them the US government may have an idea about their plan, aren't totally sure, but will keep them on their radarscopes, and if they just sail around aimlessly, the Navy is sure to investigate. If they make port at the place of the ambush, the US, with the help of its diplomatic corps, will keep wondering until it is too late."

JJ was soaking in the questions and answers of everyone then said, "Let's activate the plan and get into position at Grand Cayman." He looked at Bean and asked, "Couldn't you have just said, 'JJ, think I have found something'?"

Bean looked at him and said, "JJ, think I have found something."

"Is he new here?" Mac inquired, pointing at JJ, then looked straight at him and asked, "Are you new here?"

"I don't need any shit from you, peckerneck!" JJ told Mac and continued with, "I'll get in touch with the Board and bring them up to date. You check on the status of the other part of the plan," JJ said to Mac, as both men moved quickly toward the door.

CHAPTER 13

As day three of the Freedom of the Seas cruise was coming to an end, a yacht was cruising past the area where the big cruise ships anchor out not far from Georgetown, Grand Cayman.

The Global Express Business Jet had landed at Owen Roberts International about a mile outside of Georgetown the day before and the Team kept track of the yacht's progress as it headed toward the island.

The cruise ships anchored out in the same area each time they arrived - usually every week during the season - but the yacht could go anywhere, drop anchor, and wait. The big ships usually arrived between six and nine A.M. and departed the same day between four and six P.M., so the terrorists only had about an eight-hour window to strike.

The yacht continued along the shoreline and it looked like they might have decided to go around to the north side of the island, but then it started to slow down and come to a complete stop. When the GPS coordinates stopped changing, JC and the Team knew it had dropped anchor somewhere along the seven-mile beach.

The Team kept the yacht under constant surveillance and had nothing out of the ordinary to report.

"Still think we're missing something?" Bean complained, as everyone on the plane prepared for that night's action.

"Why do you say that?" JC asked.

"Something just keeps nagging at me, but I don't know what it is," Bean replied.

"Well, let's run through it again," JC suggested. "Your reasoning shows a very high probability that their contingency plan is to ram the Freedom of the Seas, set off explosives, and possibly sink the world's larges cruise ship, at the same time spreading Polonium 210 over other cruise ships in the area."

"For some reason, the part about the 210 bothers me," Bean interrupted. "Have to agree that was probably the plan for Miami. The ramming and setting off of the explosives would have been horrific, but the fact that Polonium 210 went airborne and spread over US soil would have been much, much worse and would have caused panic made even worse by the media."

"Well, let's work the numbers," Mac suggested. "Their target ship can probably carry over 4,000 passengers plus crew. The other ships about two or three thousand each. So approximately ten or eleven thousand people could be directly affected. That should be horrific enough to cause a media frenzy."

"You are right," Bean agreed, "but it doesn't have the same psychological value as a radioactive substance being spread on US soil."

"Good point," both men agreed, then JC suggested, "Let me play devil's advocate for a while. This is all a very good analysis, but we first have to prove explosives and the 210 are onboard. Remember during our planning that nagging question about the yacht kept coming up. Our Intel sources told us about it, we put it under surveillance, and we did intercept all of the terrorists before they actually got to the yacht. Changing course and showing up here fits right into our theories, but how about if they were notified about the Navy going to stop them, took offense to the idea, and just changed course to prevent it from happening? I know you're going to say too many coincidences, but we have to make sure before we start eliminating people.

"That said," he continued, "when the Team slips onboard tonight, I don't want anyone to hesitate because of what I just said. If you come across somebody and they get that look in their eye, take them out."

At two A.M., Pru and Met were in position well off the beach looking through the scopes of their .50 caliber rifles. Since it was unknown how many people were on the yacht, their usual spotters, Benz and Panda, joined the Team so JC and Mac filled in as spotters.

Mac and Pru would be responsible for the left side of the yacht, Met and JC the right. All were using night scopes plus each had thermal imaging that could detect a person not seen by the night vision gear. As the four men scanned the yacht from the bow to the stern, Blue Jay was doing the same thing for the fantail as he and the Team waited in rubber rafts out at sea in the darkness.

When he completed his search, Blue Jay said, "Fantail clear," into his com unit.

"Left side clear," Mac reported followed by JC, "Right side clear, proceed."

The two boats were equipped with electric motors and no sound was heard as both increased speed and approached the back end of the yacht. "Strange, no one is on watch. Be careful," Blue Jay said in a low voice over the com.

With Blue Jay and Bean each leading a group of three, the two rubber boats eased up alongside the back of the yacht. Hooks with a very strong line attached were loaded into small compressed air devices and prepared to fire.

"We still clear?" Blue Jay inquired into the com.

"Still clear," JC's voice replied and rubber coated hooks were propelled up over the railings of the yacht. Once they were sure the hooks were secured, Bris and Tic were the first two to climb the knotted rope to the deck above. Once both men were satisfied their areas were secure, they checked the left and right sides of the yacht. As the other Team members reached the deck, everyone assembled on the fantail before moving out. Blue Jay, green group, would take one side and Bean, red group, the other.

The spotters and shooters would be constantly surveying the entire boat and would alert them of any movement.

The two groups were preparing to move down both sides of the yacht when Mac's voice was on the com. "Red, man just came out of forward hatch and coming down your side."

The Green and Red groups immediately went into crouched positions. So as not to give themselves away too soon, no one looked as the man got closer.

"Looks like he is heading to the fantail," Mac advised.

Bris was ready and when the man turned the corner, he stood and fired a dart into the man's chest. Between the shock and the fast acting drug, the man was rendered unconscious before he could give an alarm. Once he was drug out of the way, a quick search for weapons was done that produced a 9mm pistol. "Man was armed," came over the com so everyone would be aware.

The two groups again got into position and after a few hand signals they moved out. Their first priority was to verify that explosives were onboard and figured since the cabins sat higher on the vessel, it would be a good place to store them for a more spectacular and damaging explosion.

As the Red group approached the first hatch, Bean opened it and slowly looked in then entered the hallway inside.

The Green group passed all hatches and Blue Jay did the same for the last one, entered, found a stairway, and the group proceeded down the steps.

After a noise temporarily halted the Red group, they proceeded to the first cabin, very quietly tried the door, and were surprised to find it unlocked. The room was dark so the first two employed their night vision gear and moved inside. After a few seconds, Bean's voice came over the com. "Safeties off, it's real." The cabin had stacks of Semtex, a favorite explosive of the terrorists, and as Tic analyzed the explosives, the others continued the search finding each cabin had additional explosives.

"You on?" Bean inquired.

"I'm on," Blue Jay answered, as he brought the Green group to a halt.

"Booby trapped and set up to be exploded remotely," Bean informed him.

"How much?" he asked.

"Probably enough to put a good size dent into Guam," was the reply.

"Be right there," Blue Jay said, knowing Tic was already in the process of disarming and Check, their other explosives expert, was with his group.

When the two groups were again together, Blue Jay said, "We'll secure this area until Tic and Check have everything neutralized then we'll see what else they have on this tub."

As Tic and Check went from cabin to cabin, the Team stood guard. Everyone knew one wrong move with a booby trap and they all would be in pieces, but the Team had been on enough Projects with them to know they had nothing to worry about and concentrated on their part of the Project.

The Duo had just about completed their tasks when JC's voice was again on the com. "We have a panel truck along the beach road directly in line with the yacht," he alerted.

"Any ID?" Blue Jay inquired.

"Can't really see; wait one," JC answered then said, "From the sign on the door, it looks like a food vendor from the marketplace in Georgetown."

"That's it," Bean said. "They're not going to let the 210 go up in the explosion; they're going to somehow get it into the food of the passengers."

"You people almost done?" Blue Jay asked, agreeing with the statement and wanting to search the remainder of the yacht.

"Almost," Tic and Check replied, as both men picked up the pace.

Hearing the conversation over the com, JC said to Pru, "Better call the SEAL."

Pru had been looking forward to an opportunity like this since the Projects started. In the past, the language skills of other Team members were required on a Project, but now they were in the British West Indies. Pru is British and it was show time.

Pru removed a cell phone from his inside pocket and dialed a number. After one ring, a voice said, "Hello."

"I say, this is Freddie Smith, the chap you met at the cocktail lounge in your hotel yesterday," Pru said.

"Hello again, Freddie," the SEAL answered, knowing it was the codename Di Flippi gave him during his briefing and knew instructions would follow.

"Afraid I'm not going to be able to join you for surf fishing this morning. Bad head, you know," Pru apologized then continued with, "However, I would like to give you directions to a spot along seven-mile beach where I have had some luck." He continued with the directions then ended with, "Sometimes another chap also fishes there, so if you see a white panel truck parked along the road, then that is the spot. Maybe we could do it tomorrow morning," Pru offered.

"I'm leaving for Jamaica tomorrow morning," the SEAL informed him, "but maybe next visit."

"Jolly good," Pru said. "Enjoy Jamaica."

"Thank you," the SEAL replied and both hung up.

"I say, how was that?" Pru asked.

"Sounded a little like Dr. Watson from the nineteen forties Sherlock Holmes movies," Mac offered his opinion.

"No, I don't think so," Met disagreed, "sounded more like Sir Sedgwick Harddick."

"That's Hardwick," Pru corrected.

"I'm talking about Hammy Haddick. That guy on the BBC that used to do comic impersonations of famous people like Sir Sedgwick," Met said with a chuckle.

"Sounds like the Bullshit Derby is making a fieldtrip," JC said, as he and the other three continued surveillance with smiles on their faces.

"Done!" Tic and Check said, as both appeared holding up the guts from all the devices that could set off the explosives.

"Let's see if there are anymore explosives onboard and especially any 210."

The two groups would again split up to cover both sides of the vessel and move forward to check out the bridge area. Moving very cautiously, Blue Jay was the first to open a hatch that led to the Green group's side of the boat, checked for anyone, then stepped onto the deck followed by the others.

The unconscious man on the fantail had been discovered, but he couldn't be revived to tell them what happened, so a search was in process to see if any unwanted visitors were onboard.

Panda was the last man out of the hatch and as he closed it, he caught a glimpse of something to his right. "Green group, people behind us," Panda alerted into the com and everyone hit the deck as rounds from automatic weapons fire cracked as they flew over their heads.

Since the people on the ship were not using silenced weapons and everyone was already searching, they immediately knew unwanted people were on the yacht. Other people appeared forward of Blue Jay's position and immediately started firing.

"Green caught in a crossfire," Blue Jay informed everyone, as he and the others returned fire.

"Red will try to move around behind the fantail group," Bean informed, as he quickly moved out of the hatch putting him on the opposite deck of the Green group. As Bean made sure no one was moving down the deck in his direction, the remainder of the Red group moved out of the hatch and toward the fantail with Bean providing a rear guard.

———————

When the gunfire broke out, everyone on the bridge was alerted, especially after someone ran in sounding the alarm. "Let's clear the bridge," JC instructed, as he and Mac scanned for targets. Pru and Met made short work of their assignments as their silenced semi-automatic 50s popped only four times. "Green group, keep your heads down, heavy shit coming through," JC warned and started spotting targets for Met.

Pru and Mac didn't have a clear view of the right side of the vessel, so they maintained surveillance of the bow and left side of the yacht.

———————

As the Red group moved quickly along the deck, Bean noticed four men had just popped out of a hatch forward, were quickly moving toward the rail, and one of them was carrying a metal briefcase. *That guy has the 210,* he thought and turned to alert the others, but they had just engaged the people from the yacht who were trying to use the same tactic as they were.

Four to one, he thought, as he quickly moved back up the deck to intercept them. *Suppose I'll have to hear a bunch of shit from Blue Jay about this, if I don't get killed.*

Moving at a run, Bean opened fire on the four men taking one down before he reached the open hatch the Red group had just come out of. Two of the remaining men returned fire as the man with the case leaped over the yacht's rail and disappeared.

Bean was again on the move and firing as he advanced. The two men were caught by surprise at these tactics and another went down from the incoming fire.

Rounds can get used up pretty quickly in a firefight and in a situation like this, who was keeping track? After another two rounds went out the barrel, his MP5 was empty. "Fuck!" Bean exclaimed, as he reached for his 9mm sidearm. His advisory seeing this jumped up to fire, but a .50 caliber round struck him throwing him over the rail and into the water.

Still trying to get out his sidearm, Bean ran up to where the man with the metal briefcase disappeared over the rail and saw him just starting to pull away in the yacht's launch and heading for shore.

Without hesitation, Bean dove over the rail in the direction of the fleeing man and just barely managed to give him a glancing blow to the head and both men went flying into the water where Bean ended another terrorist career.

The firefight on the yacht was short lived after Met and JC took out the group in the bow area and the Red and Green groups got the yacht people in the middle of a crossfire.

Everything got real quiet after the shooting stopped and Bean was treading water a short distance from the yacht when a boat came out of the darkness heading straight for him. When it was almost to him, it slowed, veered off to the right, and stopped. "Thanks for not running me over," Bean said, as he looked up into the boat.

"Shut the fuck up and get into the boat," LadyA replied, as she held out her hand to assist him.

"Now that I see whose driving, maybe I'll just swim for it," Bean remarked.

"Go ahead, dickbrain," Lady1 said with a chuckle from behind the wheel.

After getting Bean onboard, they joined Top who had another boat already alongside the yacht. Quickly loading the two groups into the boats and taking the rubber rafts and the yachts launch in tow, the boats again disappeared into the darkness as they headed out to sea.

CHAPTER 14

After the SEAL got the call, he immediately left his hotel and headed toward seven-mile beach. He checked his odometer reading and knew he was getting close to the location when the headlights of his rent-a-car picked up a white van parked on the left side of the road. *This must be it,* he thought, as he pulled the car over and parked behind the van.

After turning off the lights and the motor, he sat back, looked around the area, then he went into his fishing gear and removed a 9mm Beretta that had somehow showed up in his hotel room. Knowing a round was already in the chamber he just clicked off the safety and got out of the car. As he slowly approached the van, not knowing what to expect, his thoughts quickly went to all of those police officers that had to do this on a daily basis, sometimes with tragic results. When he got to a point just behind the driver's side window, he saw a man sitting behind the wheel. Staying close to the side of the van to give himself a fraction more reaction time if the man turned with a gun in hand, he slowly advanced and stopped just behind the opened window.

This guy is sleeping or playing possum because there is no way he could have missed me pulling up behind him. Getting a tighter grip on the 9mm, he asked in a loud voice, "How's the fishing!"

The man didn't move or say anything. The SEAL then took a quick look inside and saw the man's empty hands were just lying in his lap. "Hey!" he said to the man who continued to look straight ahead.

After Hammy Harddick made the call to the SEAL, JC had paid a quick visit to the van.

Have to remind myself not to get involved in this kind of shit again, the SEAL thought, as he continued to investigate the area. As he walked over to the edge of the beach, he could see the yacht Di Flippi had briefed him about anchored just offshore. *Now what?* was his next thought, as he moved down the beach until he was directly in front of the vessel.

He didn't have to wait long for an answer as a boat came out of the darkness heading straight for the beach with another boat in tow.

The SEAL, not knowing what to expect, knelt down and took aim at the incoming boat.

It looked like the boat was going to run aground then at the last second, it veered off to the left and the line towing the other boat was released allowing it to coast to the shore.

After watching the boat head back out to sea, the SEAL walked out to look into the yacht's launch and found a hazmat container that held a metal briefcase with the Polonium 210 plus the last shipments of Polonium 210 the Team intercepted.

Attached to the container was a small clear plastic bag with a brief note inside.

He reached down, removed the bag from the container, and started reading. *Polonium 210 inside. You know the number to call. Thanks for your help. Water soluble.* After he read the note, the SEAL smiled. He removed it from the plastic bag, bent down, and put it into the seawater.

When the note had totally disappeared, he took out a throwaway cell phone and dialed the number of a UK Intelligence officer who just happened to be vacationing for a few days in Grand Cayman. The fact that he was Di Flippi's counterpart at UK Intel and a very good friend for many years was just a coincidence.

After talking with the Intelligence officer, the SEAL dialed another number and Di Flippi immediately answered on another throwaway cell. "Yes," he answered.

"Have it and called," the SEAL reported to let Di know he was waiting for the Intel officer, then hung up, walked into the surf, and started down the beach. When he got a good distance from the yacht's launch, he threw the cell phone as far as he could into the sea, then walked back, the surf erasing his tracks almost as fast as he was making them.

Not knowing if other terrorists or their associates would show up, the SEAL retrieved the hazmat container and moved back to the area where his car and the truck were parked.

A short time later, a speeding car came down the beach road and pulled in behind his car. After going through a prearranged routine and each man was sure they were talking to the right person, the SEAL said, "Glad you showed up alone so I didn't have to tell the story about how I was just going surf fishing at this spot, found the dead guy in the truck, and the launch on the beach."

"Quite so," the UK Intel officer replied. "Afraid I'm stuck with the old received an anonymous call bit."

After he handed the hazmat container over to the other man, the SEAL got into his car and pulled it onto the road, stopped and returned. The two men then made sure the tire tracks from the SEAL's car were either removed or run over by the tires of the other vehicle. Satisfied with their efforts, the men bid farewell and the Intel officer was on his cell phone.

First the SEAL, now the UK Intel officer was in a vulnerable situation: alone with hazmat gear containing Polonium 210. Besides being used by the terrorists, it was worth a small fortune to any thieves that happened along, but not much chance of that happening, especially with four pairs of eyes focused on the Intel officer and the area around him.

After Grand Cayman authorities showed up and JC was satisfied the Intel officer and the Polonium 210 were secure, he and the others departed. The four men moved north staying on the road surface for speed and other reasons. A mile up the road, they crossed the beach single file to the surf and rendezvoused with the Team in the two boats. Using a tree branch, the last man in the column had removed their footprints in the sand and it would be hard to tell at a glance that someone had crossed the beach to the surf.

With everyone onboard the boats set off for the North Sound for some fishing, but first they would have to deep six all of the gear used in the operation. As the boats rounded the north end of the island and in deep water, they started to dispose of the gear. First the two rubber boats with motors were sunk. Then all the black clothing worn during the assault was put into weighted bags and thrown overboard at different locations. The last thing to be done was what Mac had come to call, "JJ and the Charley Tuna Weapons Caper." All of the weapons were disassembled and the pieces thrown overboard as the boats moved along.

"What kind of story about the weapons are you going to have for JJ this time?" JC inquired.

"The Board took away my fun when they all agreed the weapons should be disposed of in case the jet was searched prior to leaving Grand Cayman," Mac explained, "but I'll think of something."

When the boats arrived at North Sound, they all went into fishing mode until it got around the time when people that have been out fishing all night usually returned.

No authorities were on hand when the boats returned, just people from the local restaurants looking over the catches and making offers for certain fish.

Top and the Ladies had caught a few while waiting last night and the Team landed a few more that morning. One of the restaurant people made an offer for two of the fish and after some haggling and throwing in the rest of the catch, Lady1 was happy with her profit. Told the others she did it to keep up the cover, but the look in her eye told a different story and everyone immediately wondered what the Bullshit Derby would have to say about it.

It was a wise decision not to have anything on the jet to link them with the yacht. Prior to being allowed to take off, the plane was thoroughly searched and being satisfied all was correct, the Global Express Business Jet was allowed to depart.

Several hours after takeoff, they landed at Mercer Airport outside of Trenton, New Jersey, and with everyone loaded into three vans, they headed for the Barn.

Everyone was eager to get back to the Barn, but with a New Jersey State Police Troop Car in their rearview mirrors, the vans stayed within the speed limit until the Trooper turned into the Lambertville Police Department parking lot, then the vans picked up the pace a little.

CHAPTER 15

A few days after a Project's completion, the Board was usually briefed by JJ and Mac while the Team caught up on some much needed rest prior to leaving on furlough.

Since the last Project managed to actually become two extremely important Projects, the Board recommended the Team take a two-month furlough plus bonus.

The Team appreciated the two-month leave, but was unanimously in agreement that the bonus money should be donated to legitimate organizations that feed and shelter innocent children that have been victimized by war or evil rulers around the world.

After hearing their request, JJ told them that he and the Board would match their generous offer.

For their contributions to the Project, the Board voted to also give Dunn's sources a bonus that Gil would personally deliver. It would make a handsome addition to their retirement funds.

The SEAL was not forgotten and after digging into his service record in detail, Foxie discovered his promotion to Navy Captain was long overdue and started making people aware of that fact.

Di Flippi offered him a position at the Agency, but if he wanted to stay in the Navy, a TDY assignment to Di's group could be arranged.

———————

Still too cold to have the dinner party in a tent outside like the last one, it was decided to hold it in the Barn in the workout area. Rugs were temporarily put over the mats of the large judo area and tables were put end to end to make one long table.

Top and the Ladies with everyone pitching in to help once again had a fabulous buffet set up at the back of the room with anything you could want to eat or drink. They even had some of those little puffy hors d'oeuvreie things that Mac always talked about.

After everyone had finished dinner, it was time for the Bull Shit Derby and Mac decided it was his turn to start the festivities. "So, JJ, I was very happy to see you didn't get upset about all of the weapons that had to be discarded. A lot of money went overboard."

"It was part of the plan and a good thing, too," JJ replied.

"Oh, without a doubt," Mac agreed then added, "it's just a shame you got so upset after the first Cuban Project when I told you we gave those 50's to the Cuban Freedom Fighters or was it Charley Tuna's Gang? I get confused."

"You're going to start that shit again aren't you?" JJ erupted.

"Now, now, calm down," Mac said with fake concern. "You're going to catch yourself an apoplexy."

"I'll fucking apoplexy you!" JJ promised, as someone in the group yelled, "And the Bull Shit Derby is off and running!"

After many verbal skirmishes had broken out and everyone had finally paused for a breath, Pru decided to make an entry. "I say, does the Board have Superman on retainer?" he inquired. "When that man on the yacht tried to escape in the launch, Mac and I had him spotted, but before I could squeeze off a round, Superman came flying in the right side of our scopes and out the left taking the chap into the water with him."

"No, that was just Dick Wade," Blue Jay corrected, as he pointed at Bean. "He does shit like that all the time."

"Oh, that's funny, Peckerface!" Bean responded. "Let's talk about why you're in second place in the Annual JCCF Awards."

"Virtual Annual JCCF Awards," Panda corrected with a smile.

"I stand corrected by the man with a head that looks like a pecker," Bean announced. "The Virtual Annual JCCF Awards."

"Glad you brought up the topic," Jockey announced. "It's time for the point standings and a general announcement."

"Oh good, another dickhead is going to talk," Bean observed and everyone chuckled.

"Due to a complaint from a person that will remain anonymous," Jockey said, as he pointed directly at Panda, "the name of the Annual JCCF Awards will be changed to the Virtual Annual JCCF Awards. Apparently some people," Jockey again pointed at Panda, "are bothered because awards aren't flying out of here every year, so the name had to be changed so we don't get a lawsuit filed against us by the ACLU because of *we know who.*"

"Okay, first, the current point standings and as before, I ask you to hold your applause until the end..." He continued. "JC - 5,

Blue Jay - 4¼, Benz - 2, Panda - 1, Bris - 1, Bean - 1, Lady1 – 1, and Mac - ½."

Everyone gave mock applause.

"Now onto the updates," Jockey announced. "Two of our Team did a very brave thing, but then requested points for it in the Virtual Annual JCCF Award and we all know what that means, sooo…

"Check, for sitting on top of a mountain refusing to leave because he liked the view. Some say he didn't want to get his MP5 all wet and run the risk of making JJ mad even though Mac would probably make up some bullshit story to cover him. Anyway, while he was enjoying the view, he decided to put down covering fire that probably saved the Team. 2 points!

"Benz, who swam back to coax Check off the cliff and in the process was heard saying, 'No rush, I'm going to try and catch one of these rounds between my teeth', and was seen snapping at them as they whizzed past his head. 2 points!

"I have it from a good source as a result of their little adventure they are developing a ride, plan to market it in Poland, and call it, The Rope-N-Ski. See, that's what they did, ski, Poland," Jockey explained, as loud disapproval of the humor echoed in the room.

"Couldn't agree more," Jockey quickly sided with the group. "I think those carrier pigeons that bring me the secret votes are making stops at Cheep John's Joke Emporium. Rest assured, I'm sending a complaint back by return pigeon.

"Bean, who wanted a better view of Benz trying to catch rounds between his teeth climbed out the door of the aircraft, got onto the roof, and while he was there, happened to fire a few rounds at the bad guys who happened to fire a few back. 1 ½ points."

The next moment, the words fuckface were heard coming from the group and Jockey quickly added, "For again verbally assaulting the messenger, ½ point deduction. 1 point!

"JC, without hesitating, took out a terrorist before he could set off a booby trap device attached to Polonium 210. Said he couldn't stand to see the man destroy a perfectly good briefcase. 1 point!

"While in the process of retrieving the Polonium 210 in Grand Cayman, Bean got an uncontrollable urge to go for a swim and after taking out three gunman and a part-time gondola worker, went swimming around the yacht until the Ladies told him playtime was over and made him get into the boat. 2 ½ points."

Fuckface was again heard coming from the group followed by, "For yet another verbal assault on the messenger, ½ point deduction. 2 points!

"That brings the new standings to: JC - 6, Blue Jay - 4¼, Benz - 4, Bean - 4, Check - 2, Panda - 1, Bris - 1, Lady1 - 1, Mac - ½.

"Blue Jay doesn't seem to have any points this time, but Mac said he would be willing to share half of the prestige LBJ 'Is that guy sucking hind tit award' if he wins it. With only half a point, he has a good shot at it."

Blue Jay stood, bowed a little, and said, "Thank you, General Mac."

Mac stood, returned the bow, and said "You're very welcome. We Marines have to stick together."

"Moooving ooon!" Jockey announced very slowly, as he looked at the two men.

"At the last presentation, the Ladies had an entry, but this time, there doesn't seem be anything. Oh, well, as someone stated last time, 'The Ladies are not up to the task and it was probably just a flash in the pan,'" then Jockey quickly added, "end of points presentation," and sat down.

Lady1 immediately announced, "Another fucking chauvinist pig," referring to the last presentation when she was forced to make a similar announcement.

LadyA started to say something, but burst into laughter at the chauvinist pig announcement.

If Jockey's remark about the Ladies were an attempt to kick things up a notch, he succeeded beyond his wildest dreams. The party immediately went into a higher gear and within seconds, the volume of the group increased tenfold.

The partying went on for hours with drinking, laughing, smoking cigars, and as usual, the Ladies keeping pace with the rest of them.

When the wee hours of the morning rolled around, things finally started to quiet down, probably due to exhaustion, and normal conversations took over.

"Wonder where the next one will take us," Mac remarked to JJ and JC who were sitting across from him at the table.

All conversations ceased as everyone wanted to hear the replies.

"Good question," JJ answered. "Can honestly say I've never seen a time when so many assholes were on the world stage trying to drive everything to destruction."

"They sure know how to create a target rich environment," JC agreed then added, "We all know without finances the terrorists would not be as active. Governments try to stop the flow, but that is only affective until they find a way around it. The trick is to stop the flow permanently at their sources and I guess that will remain one of our little pieces of the fight."

Everyone at the table shook their heads in agreement and a still settled over the entire group.

www.ingramcontent.com/pod-product-compliance
Lightning Source LLC
Chambersburg PA
CBHW052139170626
46812CB00004B/1500